HOME AGAIN,
HOME AGAIN

HOME AGAIN, HOME AGAIN

by ELAINE MARKSON

WILLIAM MORROW AND COMPANY, INC.

NEW YORK   1978

M3461h

Library of Congress Cataloging in Publication Data

Markson, Elaine.
    Home again, home again.

    I. Title.
PZ4.M3477Ho [PS3563.A6714]   813'.5'4   78-7008
ISBN 0-688-03360-1

BOOK DESIGN   CARL WEISS

Printed in the United States of America.

First Edition

1   2   3   4   5   6   7   8   9   10

LD

In Memory of Lilyan

and Leon Kretchmar.

Truly Wonderful Parents.

And for David.

CHAPTER

1

THERE WAS SOMETHING SO SOOTHING ABOUT THE OCEAN. To Ella Sagersdorf, it was especially perfect tonight. As she walked along the beach with one hand in Chip's, the other swinging her Thom McAn white sandals, she thought how this night was different from all other nights.

As Miami was different from New York City. And Chip was different from Phil, God rest his soul. More affectionate. Feeding on Ella's warmth. Here it comes, a pat, a pinch. He loves me. Ella was bathed in the glow, radiant.

"The moon is pale compared to you, darling," Chip said.

"Not pale. Just turning out its lights, it shouldn't watch us kissing and hugging like two crazy kids."

Let him not stop, she hoped. God, it felt good. So lonely these three years since Phil's death. Plenty of girlfriends, but an available man in Miami was as scarce as a Martian. A miracle he came into my life when I needed him.

"Ella, let's dance. Right here on the beach. I feel like doing a waltz. Or a polka. Nobody does those dances anymore."

And she found herself moving, dancing. His arm strong around her waist, hand in hand, his voice humming "The Pennsylvania Polka." She looked up at him, as the moon lit his features. Balding, but strong high forehead, straight but generous nose, eyes shining. Could she really see them blue, even in the dark? Nice wrinkles around those eyes, smile wrinkles. Chip was always chuckling, always ready for a laugh.

They whirled around faster and faster, the Thom McAn

sandals falling to the sand after the first round. Ella giggling harder, Chip laughing and forgetting to hum. All fall down.

"Ella, I never expected to love you so much."

"Nor I. Guilty first, you know, about Phil. But you make it feel right, Chip."

"For God's sake, Ella, it is right. Irma is dead, Phil is dead. We each had a good marriage, but it doesn't mean you can't love again. I feel happy every morning now when I wake up. Knowing I'll be spending my time with you. You're precious to me."

Made her feel like a jewel. Made her feel delicate, petite, hard to believe that. Thanks to Dr. Stillman's diet, she had lost ten pounds. But she still worried about how she looked naked. Her best friend, Leah, skin and bones compared to Ella, was unconcerned. "Plump people," Leah said, "always improve lying down. You'll see, when you marry Chip, he'll be thrilled with the way you look. The flesh is soft and inviting. When thin people lie down, it's just a shadow on the sheets. Like making love to a skeleton. You, you're a sex object, darling."

And Chip made her feel like one, all right. Dainty. Ha. His caresses continued.

She did remember those paintings by Titian and Rubens from the books her son Donald had. Nice, round thighs, real bellies, soft arms. Donald always called her a Rubens mama. She had thought it was a good thing to be, many years ago. Then everyone in America got thin. She wished she were a Modigliani mother. Long, slinky, and dark-eyed.

"Ella, you know we should get married."

"I think living in sin would be more fun, Chip. I mean it, you know." She could see his frown even in the darkness. "After all, you have money. I'm well off. It's the new style. Why shouldn't we be modern?"

Ella read a lot. She knew that many women her age were living this way. Leah thought it would be a bad move. "You need to be *legitimate*, darling. I can't imagine you living in sin. I, maybe, but not you."

Wonderful, Ella thought at the time. Leah still had her Irving, so who was asking her to move in anyway? Forty-five years married, Leah was. Eight years ago, at a New Year's Eve party, she kissed Mary Bloom's husband. That's what Leah knows about sin.

"We'll talk about it some more, Ella. I want you to know that I'm serious. I'll work on you during Chanukah and Christmas. Let the holiday spirit move you. Sin is something I don't know too much about. I can learn, though." And he laughed, grabbing at her, catching her again in a hug, a very affectionate one.

Wait till she told her daughter Marcia. Could already hear the phone conversation. First she'd have to listen to the trials of living in New York City. Trying to scrape by on alimony payments. Late payments at that. Forty-one years old, and embittered. Pretty but fading fast from lack of pleasure. If Ella could send her a magnum of special energy, wouldn't she bottle it?

"Is he Jewish?" Marcia would ask. Chip? After all these years and all that brainwashing, Ella's body would reject anything but.

"How not Jewish?" she'd tell her. "But he's from Walla Walla, Washington. You know a person named Hymie from Walla Walla? How far would he go?"

They stood up again. Started walking back, the sandals collected, the sand brushed off.

Too bad she hadn't told Marcia to live in sin. Saved her from marrying Stanley Adelson. From Syracuse University to fifteen miserable years of marriage. Humph. Chip would be different. He cooks like a gourmet. Not afraid he would be treated like a sissy. He was tall, well built, strong barrel chest, who would dare attack him?

Leah's Irving snickered at the cooking. Great bargain he

was. Sitting there, lifting his feet, lifting his eyebrow, lifting his ass. Mr. Know-It-All. Nice but boring man. If he had died when Phil did—what was she thinking?—she could have married Leah. The Duchess and Duchess request your presence . . .

"What are you laughing about, Ella?" Chip seemed puzzled. The mood had been so serious.

"One of my fantasies, just one of these thoughts that wash over me, darling, nothing. But you better get me home fast. I've got sand in my tushie and it tickles my fancy."

"And I fancy your tushie, so let's go." Ella let him have the last word.

He was gone. The apartment door locked. She was left calm, soft, nicely sleepy. Reveries came floating in, bathed in warm tones. Please do not interrupt.

So, naturally, the phone. Maybe Chip calling to say he got to his own place and he loved her. He did that a lot.

Not him. "Marcia darling," she cooed immediately. "You sound so close, this is a wonderful connection."

Static. Roars and thunder. Crying, moans. Sublet? Apartment? What is all this?

"Where are you, Marcia? What are you talking about?"

"Here. At the airport. I'm taking a cab. Can you meet me downstairs and pay for it? I don't have any money."

End of reveries. *Gevalt.* Happy Chanukah and Merry Christmas. 'Tis the season.

CHAPTER 2

SHE RACED AROUND THE APARTMENT IN A PANIC. HAVE TO clean up. Turned the vacuum on in the second bedroom to get it ready for Marcia. Which one of the twin beds would she want? Marcia's sleep preparations were like some ancient ritual. When she wasn't appalled, Ella was awed. The earplugs came out of the elegant little box. The black mask went over the eyes. The pillows (two) were fluffed to the right consistency and the blonde head, in tight little pin curls, gently nudged into them. The nightgowns Marcia wore always had sleeves. Her arms were too thin and her collarbones too prominent for low-cut sleeveless models, she explained to Ella over and over again. Yet Ella wondered what difference it made. Who could take one look at the mask, whisper to the earplugs, and care whether the arms were too thin?

She raced to the phone. Chip. My God, there go all the wonderful Christmas plans. Ella did not like the high, hysterical pitch of her hello, but Chip picked up the signals and reassured her. "She's just a guest, sweetheart. She'll do her own socializing. She won't want to be with us. We'll go on just like we planned."

Ha. Chip didn't know her Marcia. She never had her own plans. Princesses didn't. You gave her an agenda, sent the limousine, and asked the footman to squire her to the ball.

Oh, God, Ella thought. And a pang went straight to her heart. Pangs come to people who deserve them. They bring disaster upon themselves. It is their own fault. Marcia was

Ella's pang. So much of what Marcia was, or rather wasn't, was Ella's fault.

She had been such a lovely and fragile little girl. Two years younger than Donald. Ella always felt it necessary to protect her from the roughness of her son and his friends. She dressed her in little silk dresses and brushed those wonderful blonde curls and kvelled when the compliments came. To Ella, it was an extension of herself. She'd never been a princess. In her household you couldn't afford to be one. She worked as a bookkeeper at the age of fifteen. Though her teachers cried to her mother (Ella was one of the bright ones) it couldn't be helped.

Marcia hardly had time to cry as a child. Her mama "made it better" before she had time to realize "it" hurt. Phil carped about the protection, about the lessons Marcia had—violin, ballet—but Ella patiently explained it was like an investment. You buy a piece of real estate, you improve it, it increases in value, and then you sell it. That was something Phil understood.

Then Ella had selected Syracuse University. Lots of nice Jewish boys to rely on as husbands-to-be.

The princess went. In warm cashmere sweaters and plaid skirts from Lord & Taylor. Shoes from I. Miller. It was important that the investment be dressed with class. On the day Ella kissed Marcia goodbye and looked into those soft green eyes, a stab of worry pierced her. She was right to worry. Marcia would choose neither wisely nor well.

Stanley Adelson was the prince. Couldn't Marcia tell from the tight little mouth how mean he would be? Right away Ella knew. The way he appraised the apartment. Noticed the hole in the Oriental rug in the living room before he assayed the antique breakfront. Said *West* End Avenue like it was a curse. East was wonderful. East Seventy-Sixth was Adelson country. They suffered the trip to the Hudson River for that first dinner and never returned. Just as well for Ella. Hated those people. Upper-class German Jews. Uptight and snobbish. The Adelsons existed but never lived, and that worm of theirs injected his joylessness into her sweet Marcia, clouding the green eyes, fading the blonde curls, draining the juices, leaving a thin (my God, almost emaciated) concentration-camp victim. But first, first he squeezed out a Pamela and a Thomas. Made sure they had those East Side names, got them into fancy private schools. Money they had for Pam to go to Radcliffe and for Tommy to spend these next four years at Princeton. Money they had for precious Stanley to marry again too, this time a twenty-three-year-old shikseh (three years older than his own daughter, for Chrissakes), money for Stanley and The Shikseh to live near Bloomingdale's. But not enough to send Marcia her meager alimony.

Not my fault, Marcia said. And the therapist agreed. Ella's fault. Why hadn't she given her own daughter that remarkable strength she herself showed?

Ella supposed it was all true. Among her friends, she was the only Jewish widow who had arranged her own husband's funeral. She made the calls, selected the coffin, told the rabbi what kind of eulogy she wanted, picked out the clothes for Phil to wear for his last public appearance. Leah said she was like a Jewish Jackie Kennedy. And it wasn't done out of coldness. She loved Phil. They had forty good years together. She did it because she had a strong sense of herself, a sense of how she wanted things to be done. Why trust the carrying out to others? But no, she did not pass this on to Marcia.

"*You* arranged my life, Mom. *You* went to Syracuse, *you* majored in music so *you* could teach in high school. And *you* were mad at me for dropping out after three years even if I did marry the Jewish prince you sent me there to marry."

"If it was me," Ella said, "I wouldn't have picked out that miserable shmuck Stanley. *I* would have known better."

But it was true, if she had been a different mother perhaps Marcia would have made a better choice. Ella never asked Marcia what *she* wanted to be. Marcia didn't have the choices Pamela had. Pam was studying to be an anthropologist. She would support herself and travel throughout the world. She wouldn't need a Stanley Adelson to ruin her life. Why hadn't Ella allowed Marcia to make that choice? Thank God times had changed.

There were nights (particularly after Phil died and before she met Chip), lonely nights when she would think of Marcia lying in her own bed. Ella always prayed that there was a man in the bed with Marcia, wrapping his arms around her, kissing those soft cheeks, caressing that bony body. It was a wish much stronger than the wish some twenty years earlier, the one praying for Marcia's virginity, the one keeping her pure and intact for the wedding night. After she got to know Stanley Adelson, she had other pangs, stabs, rents. Prayers that Marcia might get to know kinder, more loving men. Stanley Adelson had to have a crooked penis. Like his mind. Fortunately, crooked or no, it entered twice with enough semen to produce Pam and Tommy. May it now fall off in the body of that shikseh. Once, Ella found the nerve to ask Marcia about her sex life with Stanley. She had to know. "That part of our life isn't bad, Mom. He's really pretty good in bed."

Ella had glorious visions about what it meant to be good in bed. Phil wasn't big on variety, though she did enjoy the two positions he practiced. Him on top and her on top. She had neat orgasms, perfectly pitched and fairly satisfying. Only with Leah had she ever discussed the quality of sex. In the books she read and the movies she saw (especially the foreign films) people thrashed around a lot more than she ever had, and had . . . well . . . more romance than she knew with Phil. She hoped that Pam would experience some of this passion. At the same time she hoped she'd be careful and make sure the men she chose were at least clean and free of disease.

And Marcia? Was she too old to experience romantic passion? According to several articles she read, women of today were capable of more than the women of her era. Would she talk to Marcia about this? Hopefully she would be honest and frank with Marcia while she was here. They would re-establish a rapport and it would be beautiful.

Oh, God. I'm fooling myself, Ella realized. It will be a disaster. She'll be a wreck. I'll be pushing food down her throat, trying to get her out of the way, trying to include her in my plans, trying to pretend everybody is happy . . . .

She didn't know what to expect. Little pieces of Marcia stayed with her from phone calls and the brief visits. She didn't understand her anymore at all. If she ever did.

Ella ran into her bedroom to change into something smart as a welcoming treat. She wanted to choose carefully because ego demanded that her daughter notice the ten pounds lost since her last visit. She threw on pink slacks and a tight-fitting Pucci blouse. She was always careful when she walked around outside of the apartment. So many people congregated in the recreation room and around the swimming pool that you had to present the best of yourself at all times.

She rushed out of the glass doors and onto the grassy front lawn (manicured for the holidays), skirting the Christmas tree and the menorah crèche (for what else could one call this abomination?) with its blinking lightbulbs announcing not only the days of Chanukah but the coming of Christ, a message to the world from Ettinger Realty Corporation, and in particular Sam Ettinger himself, the putz.

She spotted the taxicab. Inside, in inky black sunglasses lay the body of her daughter. Ella ordered the driver to station the suitcases near the elevator, paid the fare, added an outrageous tip (why did she need to do this? Surely he would not take a loudspeaker around Miami Beach announcing the arrival of Ella Sagersdorf's daughter who has no money and whose ex-husband has married a shikseh). Then she walked back to the cab to fetch her little Yankee come home.

Marcia melted into her mother's arms. Holding her and

comforting her, Ella remembered every childhood caress. All the memories rolling over her: how Marcia felt as a baby, the smell of her hair washed in baby soap, the tiny hands clutching her own.

"It's good to see you, darling," Ella gushed for the scattering of neighbors. "What a wonderful surprise," she added, hustling a weepy Marcia into the elevator.

God's punishment waited for her inside. Bessie Goldstein, the Rona Barrett of Bimini Towers (a perfect name for this glass monstrosity). Yenta extraordinaire, click clicking her false teeth, waiting to bite. Count on her to be up at midnight! Sixty-five years of smiles wreathed Ella's face. "Bessie Goldstein, you're the first person to know my daughter Marcia is here. Poor thing had some food stuck in her throat on the plane and she can't catch her breath. We're going to sue Eastern. For a ton of money."

She waited, hoping the bait was swallowed. Bessie was predatory, but none too bright. "Marcia, what did they serve?" And from the way she licked her lips, Ella could tell she was about to launch into one of her own airline experiences. Marvelous how Bessie had an experience to match any offered up by unwitting friends or neighbors. Ella hoped they'd get to the tenth floor before Marcia started spilling out her heart to Bessie. A sniffle, a sigh, and then—thank God—the doors opened and Ella shoved Marcia out, kicking and pushing the suitcases after her.

"Sweetheart, control yourself. Nobody has to know our business," Ella whispered. As if Marcia had not heard this refrain before. Even Ella winced at its familiar ring.

She led Marcia into the second bedroom and deposited her on the twin bed away from the window. She put one of the bags on the other bed and started to unpack. There they were, the nightgowns with the sleeves and the high necks. A couple of chiffon dresses followed, an evening skirt, some princesslike shirts with lace and ruffles. The kind of outfits you don't classify as sportclothes. More dresses in this bag, and, as Ella looked, it became clear that these were not new clothes. It wasn't quite Ritz Thrift Shop, but it wasn't the latest Bergdorf Goodman window either. The second suitcase at least held a few pairs of blue jeans and T-shirts.

"Ma, I think I'm having a nervous breakdown. I really do. There was just no money. Stan is three months late again and he's out of the country. I found someone to sublet and just came. You're all I have. . . ."

Ella crumbled. Marcia was six years old again. "My baby, anything you need. I'm always here."

"Tommy went to some friend's house for the vacation and Pam is skiing in Vermont, Mom. She gave me the idea of moving back here with you. At least for a while. Can I stay?"

"Why not, my angel?" Why not? Ella thought. A few reasons. One is named Chip and he can't move in here with my daughter in the next room. Marcia had a habit of roaming about in bra and bikini panties with acres of blonde pubic hair peeking through. Where would Chip's eyes be? On Ella's bloomers? It was not fair to Chip to put this temptation before him.

Could she ask how long she would stay? That sentence would hang heavy in the air. As she brought the clothes (tightly and economically packed) out of the suitcases, it became apparent that Marcia had more than a two-week visit in mind. You don't bring *The Joy of Cooking* for a quick trip.

What was in the refrigerator? Chip and Ella were on a health food kick. They hoped to ward off cancer, heart attacks, kidney stones, and more, by eating bran and raisins, natural fruit and vegetables, and no-fat meat products. Marcia would fade from sight with that kind of diet. She needed steaks, baked potatoes with sour cream, corned beef sandwiches—the kind of food that would give Ella heartburn and return that barely vanished ten pounds.

Ella looked over to the bed. She saw the circles, the redness in the eyes. Terrible. The one thing she had given

Marcia, the one good thing, was her skin. Ella's was creamy and relatively wrinkle free and she was happy Marcia at least had inherited that.

At least. Is that a good thought to have about a daughter? "Marcia darling, we need to think positively. You need to laugh and to be happy. And I'm going to see. . . ."

"Mom, you can't run my life again. I have to do it myself. You have to let me go slow and get into shape. You can't control me the way you used to when I was young."

Ouch. This was going to be a painful Christmas. Maybe she could just stuff her ears with cotton, let Marcia say anything she wanted and respond with a smile and a compassionate nod every five minutes or so. Then she wouldn't give one of her snippy answers, Marcia wouldn't have a nervous breakdown, her recovery would be miraculous and immediate and she'd find happiness in some other apartment and leave Ella to spend the rest of her days in bliss with Chip.

"Ma, you're not listening to me. I have a difficult time relating to you when you don't look at me. Charlie—that's the guy I was seeing—you know, the one with the antique store. He decided to come out. Ma, come out means go gay. Mother? Oh, my God, he nearly destroyed me. . . ."

She's so thin with such little titties, Ella was thinking. A man who likes men, couldn't he like her too? Maybe. Swinging. Today everybody swung. An image Ella liked. She saw this big room with several trapezes. In the middle was a naked woman (always a little plump, of course). On the side was this big hairy muscled man with an enormous penis. She would swing her trapeze toward him and he would swing his trapeze toward her. She'd moan with pleasure and before she had a chance to catch her breath, this other trapeze with a beautiful woman in it (also a little plump, though more like Raquel Welch) would swing at her. Since she wasn't too sure what women could do to give each other pleasure, she just imagined the two trapezes meeting and the two bodies rubbing against each other, plump soft skin matching softness, and the pleasure equaling the earlier joy. Swinging.

Ella was alert again. So many times in the past Marcia had told her she wasn't listening. And it was true. Sometimes she didn't listen, though she could feign an intensity while her thoughts traveled elsewhere. She had better listen this time. Enough with the swinging.

An hour later, Marcia finished. Ella had hardly said a single word. The story had poured out. How did she get mixed up with this Charlie person? Why didn't she recognize the signs? Didn't she hit rock bottom with Stanley? The litany of men. *Oy.* Five years of Joes, Charlies, Bills, Eddies, Milts, Patricks (the Christians are coming). All the cures she sought to make herself feel whole. Ella pondered. It wasn't only that Stanley was mean. She thought that was the worst of him. He robbed my baby of her soul. He made her into a nothing. The Joes and Bills didn't help either, from the way Marcia told it. Frankly, she was amazed that Marcia would recount all those details to her. Limp prick. That's a new one. And balling. Marcia had a very hip vocabulary. For Ella, it was like a Berlitz course in sexual English. She filed away four or five concepts for possible future use.

There's a very real person inside this child and it's waiting, straining to come out. This child, her child, was forty-one and she better help. And help pronto.

CHAPTER

3

WHILE MARCIA WAS IN THE SHOWER, ELLA PHONED CHIP. "She's really suffering, darling. She's so wan, so frail. Listen, I'm going to take her to the temple later. There's a lecture and the speaker is a feminist. She wrote a book called *The Jewish Woman in America*. It's about me and Marcia too, I suppose. Maybe Marcia will get something out of the evening."

"El, take it easy with her. Give her a chance to relax. I'll pick you up afterward and take you both to dinner."

Such a decent man. So understanding. Maybe somewhere around this city there was a younger version of Chip for Marcia. In this place, how? If there is one, he'll be Cuban.

Sylvia Perlmutter, the Sisterhood president, arrived to drive Ella to the meeting. "Listen, Sylvia, my daughter is spending the holidays with me and I invited her. She'll be ready in a minute."

Ella hoped that Marcia would dress with special care. Most of her friends would be at this meeting and, given the subject, it was sure to be crowded. She wanted everyone to tell her how beautiful Marcia looked. Too bad Leah and Irving were on a cruise.

Out of the bedroom Marcia bounced on command and the answer to a Jewish mother's prayer. Her blonde curls were brushed softly, framing her green eyes, and the makeup was perfect Estée Lauder . . . the Renaissance look down to siena cheeks and lips. She even looked animated, Ella thought.

As she got up to kiss her cheek, she realized that the animation came from Johnnie Walker Black Label. Wonder how long this has gone on. Donald was the drinker in the family. She stocked cases of vodka for his visits in a never ending struggle to keep ahead of him.

"Darling," Sylvia sang out on cue, "you're a real beauty. And you have your mother's wonderful skin." Look at Marcia blush. Hasn't *anybody* told her how pretty she is? Charlie was obviously too busy praising the boys.

Ten minutes later they entered the meeting room. Sylvia swept into any room like an oil tanker and Marcia and Ella were enveloped in her wake. Sylvia Perlmutter was president or treasurer of every organization in Miami Beach. She was treasurer of Ella's own Bimini Towers. Her disciples chirped their hellos and the room bustled with chatter. Wall-to-wall flower print.

Sylvia made her way to the podium. Already seated there and chatting with the rabbi's wife was Charlotte Baum. Ella recognized her from the picture announcing the meeting. She had such healthy dark hair and big bright eyes. Ella could tell she was smart.

Introduced, Charlotte plunged in. Ella was amazed and delighted. According to the lecture, Jewish women were not a bunch of do-nothings. Imagine. Activists and revolutionaries. Labor organizers. Here and in Europe. Now bankers, congresswomen, executives in companies. Marcia was leaning forward. Ella was pleased to see her involved so. Feminists could be good for Marcia. Didn't they, at least, have their own apartments? She bet Charlotte didn't live with her mother.

How do you start? she wondered. How did Charlotte get here? She mentioned having three children. In Ella's day you certainly didn't get on a plane and leave the *kinder* home. With whom? The papa? Joint custody, Charlotte was saying. Better yet. She could just imagine leaving Marcia and Donald with Phil.

Goodbye, dear, she'd say. I'm taking a plane to do a lecture in Miami. Take care of the kids for a few days. Kiss.

No, first she'd have to take out the laundry, and bring it back, so nothing would be dirty. Then she'd have to cook a couple of casseroles, stock the shelves, leave a portfolio of notes. And even then, she'd be a nervous wreck, and Phil, Phil would have been reduced to catatonia.

"Sweetheart, you were wonderful," she murmured at Ms. Baum. Ella had been the first to reach the speaker's side as the talk ended. "You write, you work, you raise kids, and look how beautiful you look." She introduced herself as Ella, "just plain Ella."

"Hello, Ella," Charlotte said. "Thank you for such nice words."

"Why shouldn't they be nice words? Look what good things you're doing. Look at the faces here, how you moved them."

Charlotte followed the sweep of Ella's hand. She hoped Charlotte's hearing wasn't too good. Already they were discussing where to go for coffee and cake.

"My daughter is here too, Charlotte dear."

"Nice. She's visiting?"

Ella's eyes misted over and the waters broke. "She moved in with me. You have to help, dear. We have to make Marcia into a feminist."

"Wait, Ella, hold it. I'm not a surgeon, just a lecturer. But I know of a group down here. If you can get her to go to a couple of meetings, they might be able to help her."

"But how do you become, you know, a feminist? Is there a sign, or something? A calling, you know, like the nuns get?"

"Oh, Ella." Charlotte was laughing heartily. "Why compare it to a nun's calling? It's an individual right. We all are feminists, we women."

"You mean I am, too?"

"Of course. Have you had your consciousness raised yet, Ella?"

"I haven't ever gone to an analyst."

"Ella, you do it in a group. With other women, talking together. In fact, I think you'd be a perfect leader. Try it. Look, let me give you the name of the group here for your daughter. She can go to a meeting and tell you how it's done. I can just imagine what it would be like in your group. Oh!" Charlotte had a mischievous look. But kind, Ella had to admit, it was a kind look.

"You're an angel." Ella leaned forward to kiss her cheek.

"Remember, Ella," Charlotte added. "Today Miami, tomorrow the world."

Marcia was waiting for her at the door of the room.

"I feel so good after listening to this woman, don't you, darling?"

"I'll never be like that, Mom."

"Like what, sweetheart? Like a person? Like an independent human breathing person? Like your *own* daughter?" She glanced at the paper in her hand. It wasn't the right time to bring this up. If she knew anything, Ella knew she needed subtlety and care. But she'd get Marcia to a meeting.

"Marcia, we have to find Chip outside. Let me say my goodbyes." She went off to pat, pat her friends. And kiss Sylvia on the cheek. Sylvia always remembered whether or not you said goodbye. It was a demerit against you to leave without her benediction. Ella suspected that Sylvia had a pact with the devil and she never failed to obey the rule. In her own building, at her own swimming pool, she would walk dripping wet to the other side, to Sylvia's beach chair and under Sylvia's umbrella, to plant a soppy kiss on the cheek of the most powerful woman this side of Golda Meir. "Your daughter is so sweet, Ella. Bring her again. And listen, make her come to the New Year's party."

Oh, oh. No. Ella had forgotten. Had rather blocked out of her mind the great Bimini Towers New Year's blast. Thirty-eight men and one hundred fifty-six women. Thirty-two of the men married. Six left. For one hundred twenty-four women. Out of the six, one was Chip. Leaving one hundred twenty-three women and five men. And into that group she, Ella Sagersdorf, everyone's friend, lovable Ella should bring someone who hadn't even yet had hot flashes?

Susanna and the Elders?

CHAPTER

4

SHE STEERED MARCIA OUT OF THE ROOM AND INTO THE vestibule. Chip, thank God, would be waiting for her in the parking lot in his solid gold Cadillac. Well, actually it was light blue, but it was a Caddie and she expected that Marcia would be impressed. In that second she realized that Chip and Marcia had not met before and was relieved that she had been too anxious to think about the fact earlier. Wonderful how anxiety wipes out panic.

Rabbi Waldman nodded at her and literally slavered over· Marcia. As she looked back to make sure the rabbi had actually ogled, had actually coveted, her daughter, the rabbi was stealing a glimpse of Marcia's rear. Their eyes met, acknowledged, the rabbi sighed. So much for sanctity and Reform Judaism.

Marcia, oblivious to the lust of the brethren (Abe Perlmutter and Seymour Nussbaum also leered by), held onto her mother's arm as they glided out and into the lot. Three bleeps and Chip was upon them.

"Marcia, this is Chip, my friend. . . ." And what other wonderful things was he to Ella? "Chip, Marcia." They bumped greetings as Ella pushed Marcia in to the middle seat. And at once the cigarette. Ella bit her tongue to keep from chiding her.

"Marcia, I thought you might like to test a new Italian restaurant your mother and I found," Chip said. "It's close by and very good . . . especially the fettuccine." To Phil a noodle had been a noodle, and she hoped that Marcia noted this difference.

"Hey," Marcia announced as they arrived, "this looks like my favorite New York place. I'll feel right at home."

They were seated at a front table. Chip ordered drinks and Ella asked for her usual tropical fruit punch, which made Marcia sneer. She, of course, was being faithful to Johnnie Walker. They were studying the menu, conversation was muted; yet Chip and Marcia obviously liked each other on sight. Ella sighed, her legs parted in relief.

"Tiger!" came the shout. As Ella looked up, an obviously Italian gentleman danced over to their table, grabbed Marcia dangerously close to her breasts, and proceeded to fondle her.

Nervously Marcia stood up. "Mom, Chip, this is Tony Dappolita. Tony, my mother and her friend Chip Lowe."

Tanned hands outstretched to grip hers and Chip's in one swoop. Then the Dappolita person tugged at Marcia and pulled her aside. "Baby," Ella heard, "you look fabulous, fucking fabulous, and I do mean fucking."

Ella's gasp was inward. Her smile to Chip was luminous. Most people Ella's age have very poor hearing. Hers had diminished not at all. In fact, as her eyesight grew worse and she required glasses, her hearing seemed to improve. She had developed an uncanny sense for eavesdropping and, at the same time, carrying on a conversation. The conversation, while inane and unthinking, did, nevertheless, fill space.

"Tell me again, Chip, the difference between tagliatelle and gnocchi." As Chip began his gourmet discussion, Ella trained her ears and mind behind her.

She could not believe this greaseball was saying such disgusting things to her daughter. He was reminding Marcia of a weekend in Vermont (when did the Mafia start skiing?) and, oh, my God, could Marcia have done that? A threesome in bed? Her daughter? Two men. Eating? Cocks?

"Oh, I always get confused about gnocchi. Now what's the difference between veal scaloppine and veal marsala?"

What did she miss? He is suggesting to her Marcia that she come to his hotel and lie in his bed for a few days! Without getting up? Marcia is saying she doesn't think she can get it on. Get what on? She is telling him he knows how to turn her on. And she makes his cock crow? *Vay is mir.* She's going to call him at his hotel if she's up to it. Not if Ella can help it. Kiss, kiss, smack on the ass, the Mafia man is off.

"Goodbye, Mrs. Adelson, goodbye, Mr. Lowe." The last straw. Calling her by Stanley's mother's name! Another pig. She glowered over her shoulder at his retreating figure and could not help noticing his tight little ass. Naughty Ella.

Chip and Marcia were already discussing dinner as if Tony Dappolita had not entered anybody's life. She would try to keep Marcia from going to his hotel room to get it on or off. Or out or in. Or whatever.

Going to bed with Chip was nice. Soft, warm, peaceful, and releasing. He was a slim man but strong. As she got older, she needed the hugs, the caresses, more than the penetration. But it was really pleasant.

The Mafia man made it sound loud. Bang bang. What did Marcia look like in bed? Did she move around a lot, thrash the sheets, say dirty words? She wished she'd had a little of that wild kind of sex. It sounded better for the body than the Stillman diet.

Marcia was asking her a question. "Ma, you're dreaming. What are you going to have?"

"Marcia, I have to ask you. Since when does the Mafia ski in Vermont?"

"Jesus, Mom, every Italian is not in the Mafia. Tony's a ski instructor. I met him in Aspen."

"I thought ski instructors were Austrians. With names like Eric and Hans and Fritz. What's a Dappadappa or whatever his name doing as a ski instructor?"

Chip said that at Tahoe (she supposed that's where people from Walla Walla skied) they had all nationalities instructing. His daughter had taken lessons from a Frenchman. Big deal, Ella thought. I wonder if *his* daughter did a threesome. She squinted at Marcia. With a nod to her puritan side, she grudgingly admired the audacity Marcia showed in screwing before an audience. If that's what you did in a threesome.

"Marcia, are you going to see that man while you're here?"

"I don't know, Mom. He's awfully egotistical and boring, though he's pretty sexy." If Chip hadn't been there, she might have been more explicit with Ella. Marcia winked at Chip. He knows something I don't. Ella wondered what it was.

Ella washed away Tony Dappolita with her Tropical Fruit Paradise. Her daughter seemed to like her . . . her . . . lover. Ella decided that "lover" was a better word even though she said "friend" out loud. She remembered the song from her honeymoon. "Lover, Come Back to Me." Phil used to hum it and she thought it was their song. In that instance "lover" seemed a tame, husbandly word. Now it took on a different, a much more sexual meaning.

Chip drove them back to Bimini Towers. Marcia trotted ahead into the lobby. Ella, left alone with Chip and her lascivious thoughts, put her tongue in his mouth.

CHAPTER

5

ELLA KNEW SHE WAS DREAMING WHEN SHE SAW HERSELF IN a ski outfit. A turquoise number with lots of zippers. She was walking into a ski lodge in Stowe, Vermont. Isn't that where the Trapp Family lives? Keeping the hills alive with the sound of music? This lodge was a hodgepodge of styles. There were a lot of couches and sitting on them were a lot of men. All of them looking like Tony Dappolita.

She started up the stairway. A hand covered hers. "Ella, baby," the soft, silky voice said, "you really turn me on. You make my cock crow. Let's get it on together."

Ella's dream self didn't blush. Ella's sleeping self, however, did.

The hand of Tony Dappolita led the turquoise Ella into a wood-paneled room. In the center of the room was an enormous canopied bed, quilted and pillowed resplendently.

Tony lifted Ella tenderly. Brought his mouth down to hers and bit her lip. With what she supposed was mounting passion, he threw her down on the quilt. His fingers tore at the many zippers of the ski outfit. Zip. Zip. He pulled it off, piece by piece, down to and including the thermal underwear.

"You're beautiful," Tony said kissing her breasts. "Plump women look so soft and inviting in bed. Skinny women don't look good when they're lying down." This sounded familiar to Ella, but her pulse quickened nevertheless.

He pinched her soft flesh and brought his mouth to her navel and with his tongue began to lick it. He feasted there (even in her dream Ella supposed this was "eating") and then, from his ski pants, he brought out his own Italian salami. Or so it seemed to Ella and she marveled at its size.

"What are you doing?" she asked.

"I want you to taste my salami," he told her.

Sixty-five years of purity and Jewish upbringing and here I am, Ella gasped, in a ski lodge in Vermont eating an Italian salami. She opened her mouth. Tony moved the salami into position. She could taste the garlic, the pepper. She knew it wasn't kosher, but it was delicious. There must be more to come, she thought. Every muscle in her body was relaxed. Every orifice ready. Tony, Tony. Let's get it on. . . .

The Late Movie was just beginning. Gregory Peck in *Spellbound*. Some more snow. Just what she needed.

CHAPTER

6

WHEN SHE CAME INTO THE KITCHEN THE FOLLOWING MORN-
ing, Marcia was already there. She could smell the coffee and
the burnt toast.

"Good morning, Ma. I have a migraine."

Oh, fabulous day. The complaints began to issue forth, but
Ella decided to ignore them.

Praise for Chip did follow, however. "I really like him.
Are you going to marry him?"

Just the question she didn't want to answer. How come her
daughter wasn't as enlightened as the daughters in fiction?
Why didn't she ask if they were sleeping together? Or if they
were going to move in together?

"Are you planning to live together without getting married?
Listen, it's okay with me, and I'm sure Donald. . . ."

Does she read my mind, Ella wondered?

"We're discussing it. But baby, listen. Charlotte Baum gave
me an address. Here in Miami. A group of women meet and
they talk and they help each other, and it sounds, you know,
like it might be good for you. And I'll go with you. To the first
meeting, maybe. You wouldn't want your mother at more than
one, right?"

It was a beach house out of the pages of *House and Garden*.
This was the house of a person in the Woman's Liberation
movement? It could have been Sylvia Perlmutter's or Sarah
Fischer's or any of her other friends'. Not one piece of drift-
wood, not one hand-woven pillow. There were six people in

the room, none of them as wan as Marcia. But then they all lived down here. You got tsooris, but you also got sunshine.

She was determined to drive Marcia out onto the terrace, push her face into the sun and pray for instant health. Maybe the strong rays would burn out the problems, erase the pain.

Ella detected the faintest tinge of hostility as she took over the bentwood rocker. They don't know me, she thought. They haven't had a chance to see what a sensible person I am.

Lois Katz was the leader, Ella could see. Or maybe she just took over today because it was her house. She sat on a low hassock and directed her long finger at Marcia. "Why are you here?"

Such an impolite question. Ella was embarrassed. She hoped Marcia wouldn't say that her mother made her come.

"My mother thought it would be a good idea for me to talk to a group of women," Marcia offered.

"I'm Geraldine," a very pretty and cheerful-looking woman spoke. "Why didn't she take you to a Sisterhood meeting?"

Oh, my God, Ella thought. If she mentions I took her to the temple yesterday, it will be the end.

"Listen, girls," Ella piped in. "A New York feminist—a friend of mine named Charlotte. . . ." Already she had forgotten the last name. She tried to conjure up a picture of the book jacket but there were three names and Baum was not rising to the busy surface of her mind. "She told us to come. . . ."

"Ms. Sagersdorf, you ought to let your daughter speak for herself."

Geraldine was gentle, but the point reached Ella. Okay, I'll just listen. She called me Ms. Doesn't sound bad. In fact it sounded good. She felt like Gloria Steinem or Bella Abzug. Ella examined her body expecting some change, some notice of this new status.

Then she realized that Marcia was speaking. Oh, my God, she was telling them such personal things. About Stanley the worm. And the other men and how worthless she felt. And she's jealous of Pamela—why is Marcia telling them that? Ella felt her face burn; she wasn't ever jealous of Marcia. Not that she could remember. Maybe long ago, a little jealous of the Lord & Taylor cashmeres, of the tartan plaid skirts. But she was even then in the stout sizes and couldn't have worn Marcia's clothes.

Oh, now she was on her mother. Traitor. Remember who brought you here. What did she mean? But then it came from Marcia's mouth:

"All they ever wanted was for me to marry a rich Jewish boy. I loved my parents, they were good people. Why shouldn't I listen to them? So I married Stanley. He was the Adonis to my Venus. I got a big apartment, he allowed me to have two kids. Maids, clothes, everything. A bonus. Stan had things too. Sports equipment, girlfriends. 'Just shut up,' those were his favorite words. He always said he didn't know what I was talking about, that I was stupid. . . ."

A worm, the ultimate worm. I'll step on him, I'll kick him in that crooked penis. Ella was in a fury. Somehow hearing this—and she knew it all, or thought she did—in front of these women made it so much worse. Marcia herself was beginning to look better. Her face was flushed, her hands were moving. She parried the questions from the other women.

She didn't know Marcia at all. A worse thought floated in. She hadn't really *liked* her very much. Always too tired, throat sore, needing sprays, aspirin, Lord knew what next. She wanted her daughter to be a lively one, a clown, an entertainer like herself. Someone to hold forth at parties—like Ella did— and keep people laughing, laughing so hard they start to cry and blow noses into handkerchiefs. Marcia, never. Oh, she loved her, yes, she was sure of that. Maybe it would be better to like her and not love her so automatically. With Donald's Holly it was different. She *liked* her. Liked her better than her own two children. Told her once in the kitchen of her California house. "I love my Donald more than I love you, Holly. But I *like* you better." Holly understood.

Now Geraldine was telling stories. About *her* life, her men. Then Lois chimed in. They were all saying such intimate things. Ella didn't even say some of these words, these thoughts to Leah. And here were these strangers telling. Such stories. Clitoral orgasms, uncircumcized pricks, limp ones, come too soon. Ella looked them over again. So fresh, so clean they looked. Not one of them even seemed depressed. Marcia, however, yes, she was looking depressed again.

"I never had such troubles," Ella found herself saying aloud.

The one named Phyllis pounced on her. Nice brown eyes flashing, long thick hair in a braid down her back: "You got everything you wanted out of life, Ms. Sagersdorf?"

"Sure. I wanted to go to Canada once, Phil didn't want to. But I got my way, he gave in."

Phyllis was back at her. "He gave in, Ms. Sagersdorf? Could you have gone if he hadn't given in?"

What kind of dummy was this one? Of course Ella couldn't go if Phil hadn't given her the money. What did she think Ella was, a Rockefeller?

They all started talking at once. All directed toward Ella. Showing her, telling her, pointing out. Sixty-five years old. Sat there and let these children tell her what she should want out of life. She didn't need their advice. She already was an independent woman. Did they know she went back to work when Marcia went to Syracuse? Phil needed that extra money she earned at Abbott Casuals. Independently earned. It was an important job. She became Head Bookkeeper, for God's sake. Paid for Marcia's wedding at the Starlight Roof. The Waldorf Astoria. Out of her money. Pink and gold. Gowns from Bonwit's. The works. Paid for by Ella Sagersdorf herself. Of course, nobody knew. Ella didn't want the Adelsons to think Phil wasn't an earner like Herman Adelson. But she did it. And every night rushed home to get dinner ready for Phil. Kept that house clean. Maggie once a week, but the rest of the time you could still eat off the floors. She was doing that before these young ones knew the word liberation.

They all looked at her, nodding. Nodding like they knew something she didn't know. Lois saying to Marcia, "We hope you'll come back to another session. You too, Ms. Sagersdorf."

"No," Ella told them. "I think it's better if Marcia comes alone. I don't see your mothers here. It's not a good thing I came."

Not a good thing at all. Still, nobody was nasty to her. Then why did she feel so bad? Why the rents in the heart? Why the pangs, the stabs? Because her daughter was not a perfect specimen? Because she herself wasn't?

Marcia was walking around kissing and hugging the women. Like a scene from *The Snake Pit*. Now someone, maybe, was about to sing "Going Home" or "We Shall Overcome." This generation was always holding, touching, singing. She couldn't imagine leaving a canasta game with Ida, Leah, Sylvia, and Essie and carrying on like this at the end of the evening. Singing "Hatikvah."

Geraldine dropped them at Bimini Towers. Sam Ettinger was standing on the lawn, putting new lightbulbs into the menorah. Deck the lawn with bowls of latkes. Tra la la.

CHAPTER

7

SHE SQUINTED INTO THE LOBBY AS SHE HELD THE GLASS DOOR
open for Marcia. Out of the corner of her eye she saw khaki
trousers or chino pants or whatever they were called and the
body of a fairly young man. The face was hidden by a news-
paper but the hair was black, curly, and obviously not the
head of one of the Miami older males. Somebody at Bimini
had a younger guest, maybe a son, maybe a perfect New Year's
date for Marcia. She began to feel relief. Fade out Susanna.
The elders for the elders.

"Oh, my God, Ma," Marcia shrieked. "Look," her finger
pointing at the khaki pants.

The body unfolded itself and stood up. Her eyes must be
getting bad. The young man looked amazingly like Donald.
Not possible.

"It's Donald," Marcia added to her confusion. "What the
hell is he doing here?"

Such sisterly affection. In the last twenty-five years they
can't have spent a total of three months in each other's company. How would she know what Donald looked like now?

"Ella," from across the room. Oh, God, it *was* Donald.
Never called her "Mother." Decided years back to address her
by her first name. Made them equals. She hated it. Loss of
power. But it was. . . .

"You have business in Miami? On Christmas Eve?" Was it

possible? His eyes, always troubled, looked more so. Red rimmed. Like Marcia's when she arrived.

"Holly's thrown me out. No money, she gave me a one-way ticket to Miami. Ella, I'm sick. . . . Oh, Ma."

Armageddon.

CHAPTER

8

ST. PETER OPENED THE PEARLY GATE. ELLA NOTICED THAT the hinge on one side was very rusty. It squeaked too.

"You're Ella Sagersdorf, right?" St. Peter said. Ella looked around Heaven and was pleased to see a good sampling of the major minority groups. Black, white, yellow. Irish and Italian faces, and a lot of Jewish noses. "God wants to see you."

"It was that dream, Ella," God said, properly stentorian. "The one with Tony Dappolita."

"*You* sent Donald? Such a severe punishment?"

"I'm ashamed of you. Bad, bad."

"But, but . . . if you heard, if you were listening, then you certainly ought to know . . . *I didn't get it on!*"

CHAPTER

9

ARMAGEDDON.

She didn't remember walking into the elevator with the two of them. Didn't remember putting the key into the lock and entering the apartment. Didn't know how she got there but she was sitting on the black and white flowered print couch and the straw ottoman was under her feet. Donald was in the yellow wing chair facing her. Leaning back. Probably getting the oil from his hair on the nice clean slipcover.

Marcia was kneading Ella's hand, patting it from time to time in between her own very cold two. She looked at them, her children. She always forgot how handsome Donald was. Those same green eyes Marcia and Phil had. He had been crying. She had seen Donald cry only twice before in his manhood. Once at Phil's funeral and the other time years before that, telling his father, "You never talk to me. You never listen to me. You communicate through Mom and it's like I don't exist for you. I walk in the street with you and I talk to the air. . . ." Crying, with Phil shocked at the truth of what he was saying. No difference, however, never did anything about it. Just made Ella feel more responsible, needing to give more of herself. It never occurred to her that Donald might need less of Ella, more of Phil.

"Donald, what happened? It's Christmas, the kids. . . ."

"Holly said now. She bought the ticket. She knew I had no other place to go. Ella, I haven't got a dime. I haven't painted in, I don't know, a year. Holly herself is doing really well, it wasn't a question of money. I guess it was responsibility she was asking for. . . ."

Marcia was openmouthed, staring at her brother. All news to her. All these years, tales filtered through their mother, colored by Ella's fantasies. Sifted, collated, mounted, presented each to the other in turn. Wanting them to love each other, Ella had left out the bad parts. Each thought the other was leading the most exquisite life.

"You don't earn any money at all?" Marcia's mouth snapped shut in disapproval.

"Oh, shut up. The Jewish Princess adds a penny's worth of nothing. Did you ever work a day in your life? What the hell do you know?"

"I know a failure when I see one," she spat back.

"Failure is in the eye of the beholder. Holly is worth one hundred times your total value. What kind of life do you have?"

Merry Christmas. What presents she'd been sent. Two vipers thrusting their fangs at each other. These were her children?

Eighteen, Donald had been, and Marcia sixteen, when he left home for good. Went to Pennsylvania, to Temple University. He returned for visits, always less familiar. Mexico after that, painting. Then back to New York, Greenwich Village. At least he was close by. Jane Street. She remembered that place, that hole. But again painting. And she knew, that part of her knew, the intelligent part, that he was good. Better than good. He had technique, didn't just slap dabs of paint on canvas the way she'd seen others do. He cared, he had the eye and God knows the talent. But no motivation, no drive. Why?

"Darling, you still love Holly," she asked, or rather affirmed. "Why did you leave?"

"I didn't want to. It was she. Too depressing to live with me, she said. And the kids too basically happy to have to absorb my negative vibrations. She said that, Ella."

Good. At least no other man, no woman. Just his personality. Well, she could take care of that. It would be her present to Holly and her own New Year's resolution. She'd remake her son, repackage him and launch the new product with an Ella Sagersdorf advertising campaign.

The phone rang. Could she leave them alone together while she answered it? "Marcia, could you get it for me?"

It was Chip. Ella ran to the bedroom as toward salvation. "Help," she sighed into the receiver.

"What's this? Is something wrong with Marcia?"

"Marcia's the same. Miserable. *He's* here, my Donald. Holly threw him out. Sent him back to me. For the holidays. Chip, what are we going to do?" She heard the "we" as it came out. He was a part of her life now, he had new responsibilities.

"Look, honey, we'll figure it out. But you have to lay down some ground rules. You can't let them take over our life. You have to tell them what they can do and, more than that, what they can't."

She interrupted him as the thoughts came rushing out. "Oh, God, Chip. Both of them. Not a dime. Not a cent. I'll have to support them. I, my bill at the supermarket. Triple. He doesn't like green vegetables. She won't eat spicy foods. He drinks vodka by the gallon. She likes chocolate ice cream. He likes sunny side up. She wants poached. . . ." Back through time. Scene changed. The apartment on West End Avenue. Always fighting, those two. His room warm and cozy, hers too chilly. I like Corn Flakes. Let's have oatmeal. I hate oatmeal. . . .

"Come to dinner, Chip. Early. Bring some more vodka. I'll go and defrost some steaks. . . ."

"Sweetheart, please don't worry. Watch your blood pressure. I'll help, just take it easy. Get into a bath or something."

She could hear the shouting through the bedroom door. In the apartment next door she supposed Ida Alpert was getting an earful as well. Ida with her nice, soft-spoken son, Eugene. A dermatologist. Selma the daughter, a schoolteacher. She doubted that Eugene ever told *his* sister to jam it up her ass.

CHAPTER

10

WHEN DONALD WAS LIVING IN MEXICO, ELLA AND PHIL HAD decided—a spur of the moment decision—to spend Christmas week in Mexico City. Ella had never forgotten the excitement of the posadas, the Mexican Christmas celebration.

On a very cold and crisp Christmas Eve, Donald had taken them to a party at the home of Mexican friends. It was a lovely site, overlooking the city with a view of the two volcanoes whose names she could never learn to pronounce. The courtyard, an expansive one, was cobblestoned and tables had been set up, bursting with those Mexican crackers called tostadas or tacos (they were all hot to the taste and crispy), with pitchers of punch both hot and chilled, filled with fruits of every kind, and side dishes of wonderful sugared pastries.

Some of the neighbors presented a Nativity play. A beautiful young Mexican woman with thick, blond hair and soulful hazel eyes sat astride a donkey (Donald's friend Alex said it was called a *burro*). She was quite pregnant and was supposed to be the Virgin Mary. Everybody kept yelling encouragement at this young woman whose real name was not Mary but Elena, giggling and shouting at her as she knocked at imaginary doors to be told (it was further explained by Alex) that there was no room at the inn. Some imaginative person had constructed a small stable and the woman was led into it to await the birth of Jesus.

Phil was bored, but Ella was profoundly moved. The scene

remained in her consciousness and every Christmas Eve since it replayed itself in her head. Elena's beautiful face, how could she forget it? It *was* the face of the Madonna. She was sure it was a pretty accurate account and little Jesus, no doubt, had been born in just that way. Even then a Jewish woman couldn't get a room in certain hotels.

Maybe, tonight, she could set up a mock posada, recreate Mexico for Donald. Make him feel better. Show Chip something new, stimulate Marcia, relieve her migraine headache.

She walked past her two children who sat glowering at each other. Marcia with Johnnie Walker Black Label, Donald with his ever-present vodka on the rocks. "Be back in a little while," she whispered into the gloom.

Knocked on Ida's door. Bubble hairdo greeted her, they hugged. "Your TV was on too loud, Ella. I almost called, but you must have turned it down." Ella blushed and rushed in with her request.

"I'm expecting my family tonight, Ida. My son and my daughter will be here later." Stressed that *later* to convince Ida that her apartment at this moment *was* empty. "Can you drive me to the market?"

"Sure, doll. Wait a sec. I'll get myself together."

Ella had never seen Ida when she wasn't together. She was wearing a one-piece blue denim jumpsuit with a little heart, red, over the pocket. She was wearing her watch with the red band; Ida kept a drawerful of watchbands to match. Her hair, always carefully coiffed, sparkled with spray. Ida was a Jewish Barbie Doll—five feet two, little tight body, dainty feet. Ella always felt massive next to her. She followed into the doily palace that was Ida's bedroom. Watched while Ida put comb, Gucci wallet, cigarette case, and sunglasses into a matching blue denim bag. Spray, spray, and she was ready.

"The most amazing thing happened, Ida," she said. "My son, Donald, the artist, is down here. He's been offered a job as curator of the Ringling Museum in Sarasota." How did she think so fast? How did she remember there was a museum there? And which of her friends would know the difference?

"And my daughter came for a visit. She's between jobs." Between, all right. The last job she had was in 1958. "In fact, Marcia is going to pursue a new career."

So. Eugene the dermatologist and Selma the schoolteacher, move over. Why couldn't simple lies ever appeal to Ella? Never once could she say, "I'm sorry, I can't make it tonight." Elaborate medical plots, a dearest member of the family in particularly dire circumstances. But, obviously, only *disaster* is keeping me away.

"I have to shop too, Ella, so take your time." Ella trotted after the dainty form, careful not to thump along like an elephant with a mouse. Then she veered off, past the gourmet section, to the Cuban specialties. And of course forgetting again, so that there *he* was, blocking her path.

"Chello, missus. You still beyoutiful, my favorite person."

"Well, hello, Joe." ("My name is José," he had said, "but you can call me Joe.") "I'm going to try *your* food for a change."

"Maybe I come and show you how to cook it." He squeezed her shoulder. What kind of pervert was this? To squeeze the shoulder of a sixty-five-year-old woman. Okay, so maybe she looked only sixty. So she did tint her hair, so it was champagne blond. But he was in his thirties, maybe early forties. She found it hard to tell with these small Spanish people.

"I hope I won't gain too much weight eating this," taking down a can of very black beans.

"I love plump womans," Joe/José offered.

Swell. That's what he wanted from her. A little soft hanky-panky over by the toilet tissues. She closed her ears to the murmurs of this supermarket Valentino and selected a pot-pourri of Latin delicacies. Some cookies in the shape and color of Christmas trees finished the basket and she was ready to wait for Ida.

"What have you got there?" Ida asked her.

"When Phil and I owned our house in Acapulco, I used to have our maid cook a meal like this for Christmas. For our Mexican friends."

Ida seemed puzzled. The Acapulco house had been invented on the spot. But, Ella noticed, Ida also looked impressed.

CHAPTER

11

SHE WORKED HARD IN THE KITCHEN WHILE THEY CONTINUED to attack each other in the living room. Accepting her plea, they argued in more muted tones so that Ida didn't have to bear witness.

Marcia and Donald were evidently going through their childhood battles year by year. On Christmas Eve. Could a Jewish mother petition peace for the sake of the baby Jesus?

No, here was this Jewish mother in the kitchen. Opening a package of Patio tortillas, separating them one by one and putting them into the warm oven. She had already mashed the black beans and was ready to spread the mixture over the warm tortillas. Then she'd top it with diced cheese, the tomatoes, the pieces of avocado already turning brown, the snips of lettuce. She hoped it would look like those trays in the plaza in Mexico. She hoped it would bring back some pleasant memories for Donald. He always said that Mexico was one of the happiest periods of his life. He met Holly down there. She was working with a textile designer and learning the business. She didn't come back to the States when Donald did. Thank God she didn't have to live in that Jane Street dump. When they finally got together, they made an immediate move to England so that Holly could work with a textile company outside of Manchester. Then to London where Donald taught at an American high school, or its equivalent. Holly knew Donald for a long time, she realized. They had only been married for fourteen years. Donald had just turned twenty-nine on his wedding day. Holly was five years younger. She had long, silky, blond hair. And big brown eyes. Inky. Ella thought she was startlingly beautiful. Holly reminded her of Renaissance paintings.

So, if you count all the years they knew each other it adds up to about twenty. That's a lot of years. How come Holly put up with it until now?

Until now when I've found Chip, is what she really thought.

The tray was ready. When Chip came she'd send him to the kitchen to prepare the salad, a big one. She was gearing up for a good time. Rehearsing her number, Phil used to say. Sometimes she'd practice before the mirror in preparation for a party. Leah was the manager. It was Leah who'd say, "Shush, everyone, let's ask Ella to do Carol Channing." And off she'd go. But Leah wasn't here tonight. She'd have to plan the program herself.

Mexico. She'd be Merle Oberon in *Wuthering Heights*. Hadn't Merle lived in Mexico? Heathcliff on the barranca. Pancho Villa with the steaks and salad, *Viva Zapata* for dessert. Maybe Marcia and Donald would laugh and forget they hated each other.

The doorbell. Thank the Lord, it's Chip.

In he came with the piñata she'd requested. In this city she had sent him out to find one of those papier-mâché animals the Mexicans used at their parties. People would stuff them with candies and fruits and little gifts and play some version of pin-the-tail-on-the-donkey with it until it broke. She loved that moment when the animal cracked open and the goodies spilled out.

"You found one. It looks dirty."

"Sweetheart, think of it as dusty rose. You don't eat the paper anyway, just the stuffings. I brought some fruits and candy. Where are they. . . ?" Seemingly at his inquiry Donald entered, fresh from his hour in the bathroom.

"Donald, this is Chip. I told you about him, you know. . . ."

Donald smiled. Extended a hand. Looking him over. Can

you have strong feelings for a stepfather at this age? Ella wondered. Chip always made a good impression and Donald seemed relieved. Chip's open face, perhaps, an honesty immediately recognizable so that he was immediately acceptable.

Then Marcia, out of the bedroom looking soft and sweet and lime green. Ella could imagine the state of the room by this time. She'd heard Donald exploding earlier. Listing the items of Marcia's wardrobe and their exact locations. None, of course, in a closet or drawer.

Still, they just might make it through this evening. The kids seemed subdued, at least. Chip was talking politics. She'd have to watch that and switch away. Donald liked to discourse on intellectual subjects only: art, music, books. His one aberration was football and she wasn't sure Chip knew enough about the sport.

"Marcia and I went to a book discussion, Donald. At the temple. It was very interesting," she started.

"That's a load of shit, Ella," her charmer replied. "You don't have to sit in organized groups to be told how to read."

"Nobody told us how to read," his sister chimed in. "We already know how. It was to meet the author and. . . ."

"What kind of book?"

He would not approve. She didn't know how he felt about feminism, but she had a sense it would be negative now. With a stern look at Marcia, she said, "Thomas Pynchon. He came to talk about *Gravity's Rainbow.*"

Chip looked alarmed. "My God," Donald said. "He never goes anywhere. How did you get him down here?"

"His mother is in the Sisterhood," Ella decided. And before she could be questioned further, she ran into the kitchen and returned with the tray of tacos.

"Remember when Dad and I came down to Mexico and you took us to that party for Christmas Eve? At your friend Alex's house?" He did, and as she knew he would, he described for Chip the entire ceremony, painting such a vivid canvas that

Ella was near to tears. He's so smart, such a genius. Waste. She looked over at Marcia, who feigned interest.

Chip owned a painting by a Mexican named Dr. Atl—such a funny name, Ella thought—and he was discussing it now with Donald. Where was Marcia? Why didn't she open her mouth? Doesn't she have something, anything to add? She had paintings in her home, she went to museums, speak up!

"Marcia, don't you have a painting by Diego Rivera?" Ella pushed. "What kind of person do you think he was?"

"Ma, how the hell do I know the answer to that?"

Ignore her. "Chip, I have everything ready for the salad. You want to start it now?"

She could hardly wait for him to leave the room. "Well, what do you think of him?" she whispered to Donald.

"Intelligent, seems nice, a bit conservative in politics, but good for you. Are you getting married?"

"How about if we live together and don't get married?"

"A-fucking okay," he said. A minor miracle, that was only the first time he'd used that word with her today. "But Ella, you'll never carry it off."

"Oh, won't I?" Eyes implied passion beyond their ken. "And haven't I?" These children were taking her for granted. "What makes you think your mother's not a swinger?"

Marcia giggled. Donald guffawed. A spray of vokda hit his shirtfront. Standing up, mopping himself, he raised his glass. "I'll drink to that!" And did.

Chip returned with the salad. Steaks were ready, he informed them, and he began to uncork the wine. *Oy.* He brought wine. Could you mix wine with vodka? What would happen if Donald did just that?

As they seated themselves around the table, Ella noted the size of the wine bottle. Huge. If Donald drank most of that, no telling what would happen. She hadn't had a drink tonight; she'd make sure he didn't polish off the Chablis alone.

"Pour us all some wine, Chip dear."

She got the giggles immediately. Her toes curled. She poured herself some more and began to sing. Filled Marcia's glass. Donald was laughing hard, not too hard to fill his own glass. Ella reached over for the bottle.

"You're guzzling," Chip told her.

"Bullshit," she replied. She recognized the sign. Every New Year's Eve when she went over the edge into insobriety, it was the word "bullshit" that set off the chain.

"Bullshit," she said again.

"Ma," Marcia pleaded. "Be a lady."

That did it. "What's a lady, Marcia? Somebody who doesn't say bullshit? Someone who just thinks it and can't say it out loud? Everyone should say what they think. Fuckfuckfuck."

At least Chip was laughing. And Donald too. Why was Marcia still so uptight?

"You have a tight ass, Marcia," she said. Donald croaked.

"Maaaaa!" Marcia wailed.

In response she poured more wine into her own glass and then into Marcia's. Ella was flushed and her reflection in the mirror told her she was looking good.

"I can't drink wine," Marcia cried. "It makes me cry."

Now she tells me. Ella drew the wine closer.

Chip stood up and walked around to her seat, prying her fingers off the bottle. "Time for me to celebrate along with you, Ella. I feel like a party pooper."

The dam burst at her elbow. Marcia *was* crying. In earnest.

The phone. She rose to attention and raced for it.

"Ella darling, Sylvia. Abe and I are inviting ourselves for coffee and cake. We want to discuss the New Year's entertainment. Give us fifteen minutes. Bye."

She stared at the phone. Heard the click. She had not said goodbye to Sylvia Perlmutter. The devil would have her ass.

Giggle.

CHAPTER

12

ONE SHORT RING AND THERE THEY WERE. ELLA STAGGERED away from the table to open the door.

"I'll put up the coffee," Marcia offered.

"Hi there, Sylvia, there's room at the inn." So speaking, she pumped her friend's hand. Sylvia looked confused.

"What inn?" Abe Perlmutter asked. Perfect. He was perfect for the role of the Baby Jesus. Small and round, Abe was half the size of his wife. He wore white trousers, little brown sandals on his little white feet, a white shirt open at the neck revealing bracelets of fat under the chin. In contrast Sylvia wore black. Blouse, shoes, pants. Mary. This is a beautiful posada, Ella thought.

"And who is this handsome young man?" Sylvia looked over at Donald, who made no polite attempt to rise and greet her. Chip, however, stood. "This is Ella's son, Donald."

"Imagine, Syl, my son is down here on business and he's visiting me."

"Where is everybody sleeping?"

Only Sylvia Perlmutter would ask that question.

"In the guest bedroom."

Sylvia arched an eyebrow, or rather a perfectly penciled line: "Both of them?"

Oh. It broke through to Ella. Yes. The two of them in one room? The brother and the sister? How? Thirty years ago, telling Phil that they can't share the same room. A twelve-year-old boy, a ten-year-old girl. They had to move. No question. What good was the Riverside Drive view if a son and a daughter had to look out on the Hudson from one bedroom window? It was dangerous, Ella had heard. So they had moved away from the sunshine and onto West End Avenue for a little closet of a room, but the third bedroom nevertheless. And here were the siblings returned to mama, grown up, sexually mature, and she was back on Riverside Drive, expecting them to survive in one bedroom.

The thought was indeed sobering. It drove away most of the wine.

"Well, let's get right down to the New Year's Eve plans, okay, Ella?" Sylvia into the breach.

She looked over at Chip. Her eyes pleading with him to take over. He nodded, he always understood. Abe was already in the yellow chair, eyes closing, preparing for his nap. Donald walked away from the table; without saying excuse me, she noted. "Say, 'Excuse me please and I enjoyed my dinner very much.'" Was that too much to ask? A little speech to be memorized for the close of each evening's meal? Was it so hard to say, to please the person who worked so hard to cook the meal? Maybe Holly couldn't stand that either. Maybe he left the table in her home, forgetting to be excused. Marcia, obedient, sat at the table pouring Sylvia the first of what could be many cups of coffee.

She heard Chip responding to Sylvia. It will be okay, she thought. But my own plans, *my* New Year's, my *year's*? How long were her children going to stay? They have, and she shuddered, moved in. What kind of futures was she supposed to arrange now? What plans do you make for offspring in their forties? She'd better talk to Chip about this later.

No, she wouldn't talk to Chip later. Where would they talk? In her bedroom—what would Marcia and Donald think? In the bathroom? What if Donald wanted to pee? Or Marcia take another bath? Everything was moving so fast that she didn't have time to reflect. Time to think what this could do to Chip. Why would he want me now? Who needs a sixty-

five-year-old woman whose two children share the other bedroom?

She could cry. How—God seal my lips—how she wanted
them out. This, this, did she need? Not fights again, not what
they wanted, not how *they* feel. Chip, she wanted. Ella and
Chip.

Out of the corner of her eye she saw the tableau. Chip
keeping Sylvia occupied. Donald and Marcia near the door
to the kitchen and little sparks emanating from their mouths.
She could tell without hearing that it was not pleasant chatter.
Had they found a common argument, a subject they could
attack and beat to death as they did all those years ago?

"You're a dumb cunt." Was she hearing this? Did he say
this to Marcia in her living room? Sylvia Perlmutter stopped
fluttering her hands. Marcia raised one of her own and struck
Donald a blow across the face. Momzer, he deserved it.

"Don't you hit me. Who the hell do you think you are?"

"I'm your baby sister, you pig. Only not a baby enough to
sit here and listen to your foul language."

"I'm a pig? Look at the bedroom, the way you left it. . . ."
And into the room he charged. Ella was too weak to get up,
too interested to see whether the drama would be played in
different style by these older siblings or whether it would be
a total playback of a teen-age squabble. The language, she
noted, was at least updated.

"Now, now," she heard from Sylvia. President and treasurer
of organizations. General peacemaker. The Henry Kissinger of
Miami Beach. Let her try. See if I care.

Out of the room they flew, the bikini underpants beginning
the show. One by one he found Marcia's clothes, pulled them
from the floor, the dresser, from on top of a chair, and into
the living room he flung them. The brown see-through bra
(it was really very pretty) landed on Abe Perlmutter's nose,
the T-shirt from this afternoon fell into Sylvia's imploring
hand. The shower cap, blue with white terry cloth lining,

landed at Chip's feet. The blue jeans almost reached Ella. Towels, scarves, where did he find all of this? Was she truly such a slob?

"Ella," Sylvia pleaded.

Okay, these are your children, do something. Up from the couch. Slowly, painfully. Her leg hurt. "Shut up, Donald!" The voice frightened even herself. Donald, disheveled, appeared in the doorway. Marcia darted about the living room, collecting her possessions.

"Sylvia, my children are very tired. Donald had a long trip with no sleep. He's not usually this way. And he's very sorry he did this." She glared over at Donald who looked—catatonic —in the doorway.

"Donald, come out here and sit down on the couch. This instant," she added. And was surprised when he did. She found the proper tone of voice. "Marcia, go to the room and get it cleaned up."

"Your children should have more respect for you, Ella." This she needed from Sylvia. She knew what they should have. A firing squad with repeater rifles.

"I know, I know, Sylvia. Listen, I'll do the routines I promised for the New Year's show. Maybe Marcia will play something, but we'll have to borrow a violin. She needs to practice." That could make it better. Her daughter standing in front of all of Ella's friends. Isaac Stern, Mischa Elman, Marcia Adelson. She wondered whether Marcia could still do Brahms. Or her favorite Bach partita.

"Maybe she could do 'Humoresque'?" Sylvia had no class.

Donald was starting to mutter on the couch. Sylvia looked over at him and wiggled her finger. In the traditional bad, bad boy wiggle. Thank heaven, at that moment, the Baby Jesus awoke.

Abe, smiling, pink, refreshed. "Well, everyone, it's getting late. Almost bedtime."

Ella wondered whether he ever slept at home. He spent so much time sleeping at other people's houses, in restaurants, at the edge of pools, in the backs of cars, at the temple, could he squeeze out another ounce of sleep for his own bed?

Ella was weary. The wine was again clouding her brain. She sat down in Abe's warm, newly vacated spot and sighed.

Sylvia was kissing Chip, shaking hands with a truculent Donald, edging toward the door. Ella sprang up.

"Goodbye, Sylvia." She kissed at the ear, almost swallowing a hanging pearl. Remembering what happened when she didn't say goodbye, she was taking no chances.

The benediction came. "God be with you," Sylvia chanted.

God? Where? Again still it's no vacancies at the inn.

CHAPTER

13

"I'M NOT SLEEPING IN THAT ROOM WITH HER," DONALD informed Ella. "I'll conk out here on the couch. It will be okay."

Maybe for you, she thought. But it is not my idea of paradise. A daughter in the second bedroom. A son on the couch. For how long? Another twenty years. An eighty-five-year-old she'd be, taking care of two kvetches in their sixties.

"Ella," Chip whispered, "how about the two of us going for a ride?"

Of course. Get out, that's the best thing to do. She nodded, went into the bedroom to fetch her purse and a sweater.

Both of them still sitting there when she was ready. Stones. Blocks of wood. "I'm going for a ride with Chip. Can I leave you two alone without the roof falling down?"

From Marcia nothing. "Go, Ella. Enjoy yourself," finally from Donald.

From herself a sigh. She studied Chip's face in the elevator. "My kids kind of got to you, eh? Are you worn out?"

"Ella, I'm fine. If I'm tired it's from thinking about what *you* have to do." He held her hand.

She looked at the clock in the lobby. Ten forty-five. Almost Christmas Day. The menorah winked at the Christmas tree. Ella winked at both. They walked to the parking lot.

"You want to stop for a little something to eat or drink?" he asked her.

"I couldn't face a lot of people. Let's just go to your place, Chip."

His place. Small but nice. Jewish men seemed to need less room than Jewish women. Chip had a studio apartment. One very large room with lots of angles leading into nooks and a large terrace, a small kitchenette, a bath, a dressing room. His daughter, Miriam, had flown in from Seattle to decorate the place. Ella admired her taste. All these earth tones were very soothing. A big brown couch, a tan wicker rocking chair. The pillows were ochre, forest green. Soft. Not like Ella's bursts of color. She'd like to move Chip's furniture into her own living room.

"I'll put on some music, Ella. Just sit down and take off your shoes."

He liked good music too. Phil hadn't. Oh, he allowed Ella to buy the records she wanted and to listen to the Metropolitan Opera broadcasts on Saturday afternoon, but he hadn't really responded. Chip favored the violin. So did Ella. She would sit and cry along with the Bach partitas and sonatas. And the cello. Ah. Remembered Jacqueline du Pré married to Barenboim. Sweet girl, good musician, became ill. Broke Ella's heart. Like it was her own daughter.

Chip sat down next to her on the couch. "Here's a little brandy, Ella. You need it tonight."

Chip enjoyed luxuries. She wondered why he picked her. All the women he could have had. Younger, thinner, smarter —more luxurious. But he chose Ella. Maybe he liked a comedienne. No, he must like what he sees beneath the surface. They could talk about books together. None of the men, none of her friends' husbands, not even Phil talked to her the way Chip did. He made her feel special. Phil enjoyed her, she mustn't forget that. She was a barrel of fun. But there was more to her now. More years of finding herself, away from the children.

"Chip, I don't think I can live with them, not for more

than a few days, maybe a couple of weeks. More I'll kill myself. I mean it."

"They have problems. Your bad luck they laid them at your feet."

"My fault. What did I do wrong?"

"What difference the past? We've got to do something now."

Of course, she thought. That's reasonable. Organize. Do something. She did it before. Got him to art school, her to Syracuse. She was the conductor, she could orchestrate again. Make them healthy, wealthy, and wise. Think.

He was stroking her hair, her cheeks, running his fingers gently across her eyes, soothing her. Ah.

"Ella, let's just lie down and make ourselves comfortable."

She stood up, stretched lazily, purred. He was opening the bed. Going to the closet to take out the quilt, the pillows.

Lying down, his arms around her. Breathing gently in her hair, rubbing her back. She faced him, squeezed him gently, kissed his cheek.

"My children, Chip, they ask if we're getting married. Can you imagine, such enlightened children asking that question? I tell them we may live in sin." She laughed, wondering.

"Well, we *should* live together. I could move into your apartment. If it doesn't work, God forbid, I still have this place to come back to."

"Hmmm. Good idea. But Chip, one thing you forgot. How am I going to get Marcia and Donald out of there?"

Living in sin. She would only tell Leah and swear her to secrecy. Nobody else. Not Sylvia or Ida. If her parents knew, *oy vay*. Long in their graves in Brooklyn, they would come to haunt her. Like that scene from *Fiddler on the Roof*. Always scared her. Tevye's dream. They would find her. Point their fingers at her, shame, shame, everybody knows your name. Little Ella Nathanson. They'll know you're the whore daughter of Sadie and Morris Nathanson. A curse on you, your lust runneth over.

Yet how pleasant it was lying here with Chip. Clouds of fiddlers danced over her head. There was Ella painted by Chagall, in a white veil. And Chip, surrounded by a group of men. They all had beards. Chip too, looking a little like Jose Ferrer. As Toulouse-Lautrec. A tall Toulouse. Dancing around her the bridesmaids. Ida, Sylvia, Bessie Goldstein. Leah the matron of honor. In a long, yellow silk gown. Outdoors, a pasture, animals running around. And the clothes were old country. Why this kind of dream?

Still, Ella danced, in her white veil, holding Leah's hand, over to the other side, to the men, to Chip in his pointed beard. They smiled at each other. He clasped her around the waist and they danced. And they whirled, spun, kicked their heels until she was ready to drop from exhaustion. And spun more and more and more. . . .

When she looked at the clock, she could not believe it said four-oh-two.

"Oh, my God, Chip, wake up! Look, look what time it is."

He opened an eye. "So. You'll spend the whole night here."

"No, Chip, the children, I can't."

"Ella, you're kidding?" But he looked at her face, went into the bathroom. "I'll get ready."

Ella hoped nobody in Chip's building was up this early. What would they think? Hoped his Cadillac motor would be cooperative and purr, not roar.

Held his hand in the car. "Chip, it isn't you, you know that, don't you?"

"My darling, I do know. But you have to admit, it does put a crimp in our living in sin. There's no choice, Ella. We *have* to get married."

Did she hear right? No dream this? In the early morning sunrise, in the quiet Miami morning, he was officially proposing marriage?

"Yes." That's what she wanted. What she really wanted

all along. Marriage to Chip. Sin, shminn. The man you loved, you married.

"Ella? Yes what?"

"Yes, I want to marry you. Yes, I love you. Yes, you're a wonderful man, and yes, I want to spend the rest of our days together. Who knows how many years? Yes."

He stopped the car. She could see the towers of Bimini a block away, welcoming her home. He put his arms around her and they kissed. A juicy, tender, not so very passionate but who cares kiss.

He was smiling. She remembered it was Christmas Day. What a present. Chip.

"When do you want to get married?" She needed a date, a definite date. To get things ready.

"How about after New Year's? Leah and Irv will be back. They can be our attendants."

"Good idea. But give me a real date. I have to know exactly when."

"What about January fifteenth? That's mid month and an easy day to remember. When we're old and senile."

So. That gave her about three weeks. Housecleaning. Get Marcia set. Get Donald on his feet and back to Holly. Or into their own apartments. But out of her domicile.

She kissed him again. With more passion this time. "Let's not tell the kids yet. I have to prepare them. Home for me is home for you. . . ." And she was singing as they entered the driveway.

Bimini Towers was ready to greet them. Sam Ettinger had won. The menorah burned brightly on this Christmas morning, overpowering the tree whose tiny bulbs were no match for the extra wattage he'd settled on his electric candelabra.

CHAPTER

14

SHE COULD HEAR THE SHOUTING THROUGH THE DOOR AS SHE turned the key in the lock.

"Where the hell have you been?" Donald pounced.

From Marcia: "Ma, I've been sick with worry. I thought you were in an accident or something."

From Donald: "She's had me call every fucking hospital in this fucking city."

"So will you both shut up and I'll tell you where I was." Ella was debating. The truth would make them feel guilty. And it would leave her with the guilt in the end. No, honesty was not the best policy.

"An incredible thing happened. We were driving, Chip and me, looking for a place to have some coffee. We were waiting for a light to change when another car pulls alongside. A Chevrolet. Blue." She loved to add small details.

"Chip looked over and grabbed my hand. The people in the next car were from his home town and he hadn't seen them in five years. Imagine. So he starts to honk and they look over at us. Then the woman is shrieking and Chip is shouting that we should all stop and have a drink together. So we pull into the nearest hotel. Their names were. . . ." She was a little tired and it was hard to make up such a complicated story.

"Gert and Eli Goldsmith. They're from Seattle. He's a professor at the university. She was Chip's cousin. Well, she still is, of course. They were very close and we were sitting there and reminiscing about the years past and about Chip's wife, may she rest in peace, Irma. They still see Miriam. That's Chip's daughter who lives in Seattle. We had a lot of drinks and coffee and decided to have some deli and nobody knew it was so late. And. . . ."

Donald yawned. Marcia was enthralled. She'd always loved Ella's stories, even as a child. Ella could see that Donald was finished with her, however. As long as she was alive, her son gave up caring.

"Ma, I woke up about three to go to the john," Marcia was saying, "and your bedroom door was open. You must have forgotten to close it. . . ."

No she hadn't. She clearly remembered shutting the door. Tight. Why was Marcia lying to her? Had she been coming into her mother's room? Like when she was a little girl?

"She woke me. Some puerile suggestion about your demise." Really, Donald did not have to be so mean. He couldn't say a kind word to Marcia.

"Well, I'm fine. Don't I look fine?" She faced them. Beseeching. "Let's all try to get a few hours' sleep. It's Christmas Day. It will be quiet, okay?"

She threw kisses at them, then closed her bedroom door. Tight. Took off her clothes and turned on a small lamp. Walked over to the full-length mirror on the closet door and looked at herself. The early morning light was flattering. There was the patina of a sculpture about her body. The thighs were strong, the folds of the belly were like interestng lines on the marble. It didn't look as bad as she expected it would. She tried to lie down on the bed and catch that reflection in the mirror. She had to use both pillows to prop her head so she could see. Well, Leah had a point. Lying down was better than standing up. This is what Chip would see. She'd use a bathrobe or nightgown when she got up from the bed. Chip was so slim in comparison to her girth. Even with ten pounds off, she was no sylph. Still, she was relieved that the picture would be interesting for Chip.

Her body she could disguise. The two people in the apartment she couldn't hide. Maybe if she soaked in a tub, she could figure out what to do.

She ran some water, thankful that there was a second bathroom. She sank slowly into the tub.

Problem Number One: Marcia. Okay, inside that daughter of mine is a hidden personality. I'll find out what she wants to do. No, better, a flash of light: Lois from the women's group. Maybe Lois can help find her a job and if she gets a job, she can get an apartment. I'll promise her the black and white couch and the yellow chair. She can have some of my pots, anything she wants. Already she was starting to feel better.

Still, she had to proceed carefully. She couldn't be a dictator. Does Marcia have any skills like typing or shorthand? Executive secretaries got a lot of money. And get her a roommate. You could find a larger apartment if you had another person sharing the rent.

She turned on the tap to add more hot water. Problem Number Two: Donald. Harder, more resistant. A fact. It was the same when he was twelve. You had to come at him from an angle. Obliquely. And worry about his pride. Okay, he was a painter who didn't paint. Find him a gallery in Miami to show his past work? Good. Sell some and put his pride back.

Supposing she printed up cards? Donald Sager, Artist. Works displayed. Maybe in the newsletter from the temple. Or in the Bimini Towers *Bugle*. How about portraits? Do married couples. Let Donald Sager get you on canvas before one of you dies.

And he's so smart, why couldn't he teach? Lots of colleges, junior colleges down here; she could sneak some applications from California schools too, fill them out, get him closer to Holly. Ella was sure everything would improve with Holly if Donald were only working. . . .

The water was soothing. But it was time, she guessed, to face the fact that her children were in a very bad way. Real problems. Who would want to live with these two meshug-geners? Could she truly make them healthy in three weeks?

Leah's daughter lived in Miami with her husband. Ella remembered Terry talking about family therapy, about going to a psychiatrist with her husband and the two kids. Terry's kids were fourteen and eleven, but does a therapist discrim-inate? A family is a family, no?

The only problem, a major one, was time. The day after Christmas, she'd start. Call the women's group, get the doc-tor's number, find out about applications for the college jobs. It was a long time since she'd had this much to plan. Again, her spirits began to soar. Ella was feeling noble.

Wrapped in a bath sheet she returned to the bedroom. And didn't Gladys Siegel have a son who taught at the uni-versity? One more call she'd make.

Holly she'd call also. To have kicked him out at this time of year, how bad things must have been. Yes, Holly also.

Ella hugged herself. Pleased with her agenda, with the course of action she'd planned. No way to fail.

She opened the bedroom door quietly. Pulling the towel tighter, she tiptoed to the kitchen to make some herbal tea. Her curiosity drew her to the couch. He was sleeping. So sweet. Donnie. That's what she called him when he was a little boy. He was a nice kid. Look at that brow, frowning in sleep. Look at those lashes. Gorgeous. Very gently she touched his cheek. He didn't move.

"I love you, Donnie," she sighed, stepping over his desert boots, over the white sox, over the khaki trousers, and into the kitchen. Motherlove. Spare me.

CHAPTER

15

SOMEHOW THEY GOT THROUGH CHRISTMAS DAY. DONALD found every football game on every channel, his pacifier for the afternoon.

Sylvia delivered a violin for Marcia also, and she went into the second bedroom, closed the door and played. Ella managed to listen. Rusty, but not bad, not bad at all. And when Ella contrived a pretext to wander in, even her face was different. Transformed. No pout, no tears. Ella and Brahms together, just the combination to mold Marcia into a person of quality.

Eight A.M. 'Tis the day after Christmas and all through the house not a creature is stirring. Only me, she sighed. Putting up water for the coffee. Tiptoeing through the living room, now filled with the odor of stale cigarettes. She wondered how early she could call the psychiatrist. Dr. Kramer. Maybe some families got an early start and he'd be in session.

She took a big mug of coffee into her room. Dialed the number.

"Dr. Kramer? I'm a good friend of Terry Lewis. Yes. She recommended you quite highly. I'm a widow and having problems with my son and my daughter. Terry thought you could meet with us. It's really a life or death situation." Make him care.

"You do have time for me? That soon? Well, it is lucky you can give me an hour this afternoon. No, no. They're home. No problem. See you at three."

No problem. Only one. How to get Marcia and Donald to go with her.

Marcia spent most of the morning sunning on the terrace. Donald went down to the pool. He'd be the only one swimming in it. Maybe some of the grandchildren visiting for Christmas. He'd love that. Breaststroking with some ten-year-old snot-nose. She'd hear about that from him. Like it was her fault. Maybe he did that to Holly too. Donald's assumptions, she called them. The world was out to screw him. Not the whole world—well, maybe yes. A dybbuk, a little genie perhaps. God would send this figure to thwart and destroy Donald Sager. As if God had nothing better to do with His time.

She'd get Dr. Kramer to talk to him about this. Why was he always mad at the world? Mom, look what *you* did. But she hadn't done anything, usually. Sometimes, cleaning, she put a picture, a book, in the wrong place. A crime. Destroyed his karma. Zen Jewish. How she hated that, glad to be destroying his karma. Stomp, stomp, she clumped around his adolescent bedroom.

Children put a Jewish mother through a lot of tsooris.

She brought the hot bagels to the lunch table and sat down.

"Listen, I haven't wanted to worry you, but I've been seeing a doctor recently and"—before they could interrupt she'd get it all out, holding up her hand like a traffic cop—"he said he'd like to see both of you with me this afternoon."

Instant attention from her children.

"Ella, why didn't you say . . . ?"

"Ma," Marcia added, "I didn't know anything was wrong. You look so good. . . ."

"Don't worry," she told them. "I think it's all in his head."

CHAPTER

16

AND IT CAME TO PASS, WHEN THE THERAPIST AROSE, AND
came and drew nigh to meet Donald, that Donald hastened,
and ran to meet the Therapist. And Donald put his hand in
his bag, and took thence a stone, and slung it, and smote the
Therapist in his forehead; and the stone sunk into his forehead,
and he fell upon his face to the earth. So Donald prevailed
over the Therapist with a sling and with a stone.

—Ella, IX, 13

"Ma, I swear, it's the first time in thirty years I agree a
hundred percent with Donald. Those tiny little tables and
chairs? And building blocks? And children's games?"

"Marcia, so I was misinformed. There's somebody you
know in this world who's perfect?"

CHAPTER

17

SHE KNOCKED ON IDA'S DOOR.

"Hi, Ella, come on in a minute." Ida was always ready for company. She spent her days preparing for the possibility. Today she wore flowered silk pants and a bright blue nylon shirt. The hair, as ever, was sprayed stiff. On her feet she wore gold slippers. Cinderella awaiting the ball.

"Listen, Ida, how about coming in for coffee and cake tonight? With my kids and Chip. And you can do a favor for me. You know my Donald is a painter. Well, he's a really good one. He does portraits too. He's done some very famous people in Hollywood. Paul Newman. Warren Beatty. Art Carney." Threw that one in for the older set.

"How would you like a portrait painted to frame and put over there?" She pointed at the mantle over the fake fireplace. Ida had been looking for almost a year for an "arrangement" to grace that blank wall. Ella saw the eyes gleam beneath the black mascara.

"He's really good, Ella?"

"Ida, he's won prizes. He did Joan Crawford, Joanne Woodward. Think how he'll capture your beauty. I know he could." Ella tried to envision the finished painting. She gave up. Could she convince Donald to avoid abstraction?

"It would only cost one hundred dollars. That's dirt cheap and I'd have to swear you to secrecy. Don't ever tell anybody I gave you this special price. If you *want* the portrait, of course."

Ida looked at the blank wall. Ella could see she was estimating the value. Any other arrangement would cost twice as much.

"So why not?" She agreed.

"Now, listen. He's a funny kid. You know how painters are? Well, make like it's your idea. When you sit down for the coffee say, 'I hear you're a painter,' something like that. Say how much you've always wanted to have your portrait painted. I'll take it from there. Ida, please remember, it's not my idea."

"Ella, I'm not a dummy. What time do you want me to come?"

"We'll eat about seven. Say seven-thirty."

"So late?" Ida wailed.

"Well, we usually eat earlier. But with Marcia and Donald here, Ida, it isn't chic. So we wait. Actually, I like it. You eat better, you're hungrier." Ella smiled at her.

"Come and look at what I'm wearing New Year's Eve," and she pulled Ella into the bedroom. On the white chenille bedspread lay yards of chiffon. Peach. It was a pretty color. Ida would look lovely. But for whom? The other one hundred fifty widows? Maybe one of the five eligible men would comment. Couldn't doctors, maybe one scientist, find medicine to keep men alive just a little longer?

She hadn't begun to prepare for New Year's. And she wanted to look especially nice for Chip. She should also start thinking about a wedding dress. She'd go to Jordan Marsh or maybe a small boutique. Better do it tomorrow. Or maybe wait? The January sales, she'd get a real bargain.

When she entered her own apartment, Marcia was standing near the phone. Face like a Cheshire cat, grinning. "Ma, I won't be home for dinner tonight. I have a date."

"Anyone I know?" she whispered, afraid of the answer.

"Yeah. I won't be in early, so don't wait up for me. Do you have a key I could take?"

"Here, take this one, I have another set hanging in the kitchen." Next to the salami.

"I'm going to bathe now, Ma, and gargle for my throat.

I'd like to get an earlier start. Maybe I'll walk around a bit. Listen, I hate to ask you, but can you spare a couple of bucks?"

"Of course, sweetheart, let me get my purse."

She should slip Donald a few dollars too. She'd better get to the bank tomorrow and get some cash. Do it in a subtle way. Give each one money so the other doesn't notice. Anyway, it will be better to have Marcia away when Ida comes. No flack. What if Donald wants to go out too? She'd have to beg, keep him home.

Chip arrived early with another bottle of vodka. Thank goodness, she was running low. Donald didn't have the glass out of his hand for a minute. Why he didn't fall down drunk she couldn't figure out.

She walked into the bedroom. This was a good time to call California. Donald was occupied with the early news and Chip would keep him company. She dialed hoping everyone was home.

Lizzie answered. "Sweetheart, it's Grandma Ella. How are you, darling?" She was told, blow by blow. "Let me talk to Janet and then you can put Mommy on. Is she home?" Good, everyone was there. Holly closed the office for two weeks every Christmas. She came to the phone after Janet had finished her twelve rounds of kisses.

"Holly, how are things?" Not waiting for an answer, Ella gushed, "He's a mess, he misses you and the kids so much. . . . What do you mean you don't believe it, do I lie? . . . He cried on Christmas Day, really, Holly. If this separation is temporary, will you take him back if he's changed?" She listened hopefully, heard only a pause, plunged on anew.

"I think he's drinking less." (A real lie.) "We haven't talked too much about what he's going to do. But he understands he has to do something. I think he'd like to teach. No, he *has* mentioned it. We haven't pinned him down, but I think that seems to be his plan. I think he'll do anything to make himself special in your eyes again, dear." Well, that also was true. "I just wanted to know if there was a chance. You don't have . . . well, another man, a boyfriend? . . . No, darling, I really didn't think so. And I understand. Yes I do. I knew you loved him. He failed you as a person? He's failed me too, dear. I expected he'd make more out of his life. Maybe you make it too easy for him. No, no, I don't mean it against you, dear, I'm just trying to get information so I can help. I'm not butting in, Donald would hate that, but maybe I can do a little spadework, you know, see what's around for him. . . . Yes, here in Florida. Yes, I understand you don't want him running back yet. Of course, he should grow up first. He knows that too. Space and time? Just what you both need."

Bullshit. Where will he find the time? The space he found already. In her living room. "Frankly, Holly, and don't say anything if he calls you. . . . Oh, you won't talk to him? Well, okay. But if you do, don't say what I'm telling you now. Chip, that's the man I've been seeing, Chip and I are getting married on January fifteenth. Yes, I am very, very happy. But I have to get Donald and Marcia out on their own. . . . Oh, Marcia. Well, she's down, too, for a temporary visit. A long one. Yes, it is pretty hard for me. No, I'm all right. Holly, darling, don't let this affect you. I really understand what you've been telling me. I know you're a smart girl, that you know what you're doing. And you know my Donald better than I do. Holly, let me tell you. If it doesn't work out, if you don't get back together, I want you to know that I really do love you. You and the girls. You're precious to me." The tears came, the flood. She needed to do this to Holly? She felt awful. "Darling, I'll call you and you call me. Collect, anytime. I know you don't have to call me collect, but do if you want. I'm saying you can. Take care, darling, and call me."

She went to the bathroom and bathed her eyes with Murine. Put on some blue mascara, brushed the hair, and went inside.

She was removing the plates from the table after dinner

when the doorbell rang. "Chip, can you get it for me, please?"

Waves of perfume preceded Ida. Introduced to Donald. Pleasant smiles all around. Chatter, chatter. Get to it, Ida, her eyes pleaded.

"I'll bring in the cake and coffee. You'll have some, Ida, right?"

"Sure. Oh, Donald," she saw the message in Ella's look. "I wonder if I could ask a favor. You're a painter, aren't you?"

Donald nodded. Eyes hooded.

Ida began the flirtation. "I have always wanted, all my life, to have my portrait painted. Your mother said maybe, if I asked you. If while you were visiting, well, do you think it's possible? I'd pay for it, of course."

He looked at her again. "Possible, yes. But I don't like to be told how to paint. Would you be willing to let me do it my way?"

"As long as I don't look too terrible," her eyes begged for a rejoinder. Say I'm beautiful.

"You're such a good-looking woman, Ida," Ella managed to say. "How can he help but make you beautiful?"

"Not a bad idea, actually," Donald said aloud. "In fact, I might enjoy it. We could start tomorrow morning, if it's okay with you. You've got to give me some sittings."

Ella had forgotten that. He was going to sit and talk to her friends. God knew what he would say. Like the character in *The Ancient Mariner*. Had to tell everybody his tale. Tsooris lists. My wife supports me, so forth and so on. He would tell any stranger the most intimate details. . . .

Still, why didn't he start on Ida tonight? Then she'd have some time alone with Chip.

"Ida, I have a wonderful idea," Ella said. "Why doesn't Donald paint you in the New Year's Eve dress? You could put it on and I'll send Donald in. She has very good light in there, better than I have. What do you think?"

"I guess I could, Ida. I've got a sketch pad with me, I'll go get it."

"And you know what, sweetheart, maybe Chip will drive you to the art supply store to get the paints tomorrow."

"It would be a pleasure, Donald." Count on Chip.

"Well, it's all set. Isn't that wonderful, Chip? My Donald is going to paint one of my dearest friends in the world." She smiled broadly at Ida.

"Did you tell the kids yet?" Chip asked as soon as Donald and Ida left the apartment.

"Wait, we have to wait. They'll feel too guilty if I tell them now. You see how I'm organizing. He'll be okay. I'll start on the applications for college tomorrow. Can you drive me?"

"Drive where?"

"Around to the colleges, to get applications for teaching jobs."

"Are you sure they use applications, Ella? And what if he gets wind of what you're doing? He'll back off and you'll be in a worse pickle."

"I know how to handle this. Don't worry. I just need to be driven. I don't think I could find all the places with a taxi."

"And Marcia," Chip asked, "what about her?"

"I'll take care of her later. When she comes home from her . . . date. We'll sit, I'll suggest. I'll take care of everything. By the fifteenth, I promise, this place will be ready to receive you."

Lecherous might have been the word for her grin. He reached over to kiss her.

She could hear Donald's snores through the bedroom door. "You sleep there and Marcia will take the couch tonight." He had agreed readily.

It was nearly two in the morning and she was very tired. The Late Movie was a bore. Made for television, slow moving. She wished they had run a good old film. A Bette Davis movie. *Jezebel* or *Old Acquaintance* or *The Old Maid*, or maybe that marvelous one with the Lane Sisters and John Garfield and Claude Rains. Instead, a blind detective. Who could believe such crap?

At last the key turned in the lock. In she came. Not too bad, doesn't look like she's been through it. Did she get it on? Ella wondered.

"Ma, why are you up so late?"

"Just thought I'd wait and talk to you. You know, a serious discussion, just the two of us. Donald's asleep." His snores continued to ring through the closed door in case Marcia had any doubts.

"What do you want to talk about at this hour? That can't wait till tomorrow?" She yawned.

"Darling, we can't keep putting off till tomorrow. Scarlett O'Hara did that and she lost Rhett Butler." Good point, Ella told herself.

"What's that got to do with anything?" Obviously, Marcia didn't agree.

"Look, we have to make decisions about your future."

"Now, at two in the morning? Don't you think we'd make better plans at ten in the morning? Over coffee?"

"I have a little coffee now, if you want me to heat it?" Ella offered.

"Okay, Ma, you're serious." Marcia reached down and removed her shoes. That was considerate, Ella felt. Another child, somebody else's daughter, might have kicked them off to make a loud thump, thump on the floor. To disturb Marvin Silverman—if he was sleeping in his living room. Gee, come to think of it, Marvin was about forty-five. She'd forgotten about him. An executive with Burdine's. Single. Not bad looking. Slight nasal condition, always drip, drip, but so what? And so close by.

"Tony Dappolita, you went to bed with him?" No further preface necessary.

Marcia smiled. "Actually, Ma, I wouldn't have minded, but we didn't. Tony wasn't in the mood. He wanted to dance and we did. I'm pooped."

Could she be telling the truth? When Marcia was younger,

Ella believed you could tell by the eyes. A little glazed meant you know what. It was harder to tell now. She looked clear-eyed though tired. Well, you could be tired from hanky-panky too. It wasn't only dancing that wearied a person. Maybe she could sit close and sniff her cautiously. If she smelled clean and fresh, that meant a shower in someone's bathroom. And she knew the odor of her Dial soap. She moved closer to Marcia. All she sniffed was a faint underarm odor. Probably from sweat. From dancing.

"How long can you go on like this, Marcia?" Not the best question for two in the morning, Ella realized, but certainly to the point.

"I suppose as long as there's nothing else in my life. Got any suggestions, Ma?"

"I don't know a lot of things about you, Marcia. I mean now. I remember a lot from your childhood. I don't know what you do, if you can type, take shorthand, did you ever take special courses? I've no idea. It embarrasses me a little, but maybe I'm not the only mother who doesn't know. . . ."

"Ma, you're a good mother. Don't beat yourself. You probably can't tell it from me, and from Donald, we're not such swell reflections. But we do love you. Honestly. A lot of what we are has to do with the times and not you."

"Sweetheart, I am proud. I don't deserve this. But I wanted to talk to you about *doing* something with your life. A job, I don't know, even to try a career."

"It's hard to solve, Mom. I still like music, but I don't have the credentials to teach. And I'd probably make no money working in someplace like a record store. I do know that I can't afford to wait for someone else to take care of me. I'm thinking, but I have to take my time."

Sure, she thought. Take a week, the most, and remake your life. Was it possible? Not terribly.

"I'm not a very interesting woman, Ma. I see that. God knows, Donald makes the point constantly. He doesn't think I'm hot spit, now does he?"

"Well, sibling rivalry. Brothers never see their sisters as

people. I have brothers. I know how it is. Okay, they didn't scream at me the way Donald screams at you. We kept it inside. In those days. Did I ever tell you how angry I was I couldn't go to college? They went, but not me. I'm not as smart as your uncles? Tell me the truth, who's smarter?"

"Ma, you are. They aren't so special."

"What do you mean, Marcia? Our family is *very* special. Better than the Adelsons. Better than that Stanley, I'll tell you."

"Ma, you don't have to tell me. Anything is better than the Adelsons." She giggled. Looking better every day. Maybe Ella should go to the women's group with her once more, be sure she was on her way. See that the other women understood how maybe she was a little behind them in chutzpah, but that she came from a forward-looking family.

"Ma, I'm fading fast. Let's turn in, okay?"

"Listen, Marcia, I've got a big bed. Queen size. Why don't you come share with me tonight? Maybe we'll give each other strength."

"I'd like that. Boy, it's been a long time. Remember the night before I was married? You put Daddy in my bed and you and I shared yours. We talked and you held me like a baby. I never forgot that, Mom."

It was three o'clock now. Ella went into her bathroom to wash up and put on her nightgown. Thinking again about the night before Marcia's wedding. Nice. Talk again and wrap her arms around her baby.

So there she lies, long-sleeved nightgown, earplugged and masked, the beautiful dreamer. Mazeltov.

CHAPTER

18

MORNING? A DREAM SHE MAYBE HAD? BECAUSE THERE WAS no daughter in the bed next to her now, not even that mummy. Instead, shouting from the living room. Nasty. Everything, they knew how to spoil.

A head peered in. Donald. He saw that she was awake.

"I'm going swimming in your fucking pool and I don't know when I'll be back. I want to get away from this goddamn family. Chip is taking me to the art store later. I'll meet him downstairs. You got some cash you can lend me? I'll pay you back with Ida's money. How much did you tell her I charge?"

"Here's money. I told her one hundred, but only for her. She should tell anyone who asks a hundred fifty."

"God, these people can afford more than that."

"Donald, they can't, most of them. They have a set income and it doesn't go very far these days. Most of these people you think are rich live from hand to mouth. I'm not saying I do, 'cause I'm not broke. But the market isn't helping me and prices go up all the time."

Give him something to think about.

"Tell you what, I'll leave my key at the desk downstairs if I'm out when you come back. Listen, Donald, I meant to ask you. What style are you using for Ida?"

"What?"

"You know what I mean. Obviously, you aren't doing her abstract or cubist like Picasso. Will it be very realistic or maybe *impressionistic*?"

"You're *telling* me, Ella. You're not asking me. I'll do it
nice. Don't worry. You'll be able to hold up your head among
your friends. I'll make Ida so gorgeous they'll give her a movie
contract. Is that cool?"

"You got the drift, eh?" Ella loved to talk like the Fonz
from TV. Donald did not seem to get the reference. Could
it be he didn't watch? He left the room. She sighed, burrowed
under the covers, and shut out all sounds.

The door opened anew. Marcia flounced in. "Ma, I can't
stand him. It's easy to see why Holly kicked him out. He's
such a bastard."

"Marcia, he's going out. Relax for a while. What are you
doing today?"

Eyes blank. Obviously nothing. That kind of look with no
plans. "Maybe you should call that Lois. She was such a
nice girl. Woman, I mean."

"I don't really know her. And I don't like to push myself
on people. I'll go to the next meeting. I just can't get on the
phone the way you do, Ma."

Ella did it all the time. What's such a big deal when you
want something done or when you want to get to know a
person? You pick up the phone. She couldn't remember
whether Lois had Marcia's phone number. Yes, vague memory
of leaving it on a slip of paper. For the FBI files. She'd love
to have her name on a list in Washington. As a revolutionary,
imagine how proud the grandchildren would be. Her own two
children, they'd have heart attacks. Too bad she hadn't joined
the women's liberation movement during the Nixon years.
Maybe the police would have beat their way into her apartment. She'd show them, be ready and waiting. Sewing her
American flag just like Pat Nixon.

"Marcia, you should do something today. Not just sit
around. You could practice the violin. Go out on the terrace."

"Maybe I'll go shopping."

She didn't mean the supermarket, Ella knew that. She
meant department stores. That meant money. Should she

mention it? Pretend it wasn't a problem? Certainly it wasn't a problem for Marcia. Not if her mother paid. Unfair, Ella. The poor girl is going through hard times.

"Keep the key I gave you yesterday. Come and go as you please."

She closed the door after Marcia, went into the bathroom to prepare. She had to look, well, elegant. She was going to see the head of the Art Department at the college to try and push Donald; it wasn't going to be easy.

She brushed her hair to look like a retired professor. That's what she'd say when she got there. First she had to get through Jeff Siegel's friend. His name was Sy (Seymour, she was sure) and he taught something called Renaissance Studies. He was the one whose friend was head of the Art Department. Sidney George. Two first names and no last name. Probably dropped Cohen from the amalgamation.

Opened the closet. The dress should be conservative. Also something to go with white gloves. She had to wear white gloves. If not, they'd know she was never a teacher, a professor. Little pearls, a pin, navy blue pumps, a shoulder bag to match. That's right. No hat, just look casual, collegiate. No sandals, no pink trousers, no Pucci shirts, no white beaded sweaters. Never on the back of Ella Sagersdorf, academician extraordinaire. Already she was beginning to feel smarter, more intellectual. Ella could really get into a part, really feel the role.

Applied her makeup very carefully. Just a faint hint of blue eyeshadow. Even gentile women used eyeshadow. Maybe she'd look like a Wasp lady. Maybe Sidney George would think so. Ella giggled aloud. What a gas.

The house was quiet. Always quiet now with one sibling gone. Together in the house, it was like living in a hurricane zone. . . . A brother, a sister, at this age they should sit together without fighting. Couldn't say pass the bread without an explosion. Where did they learn to behave like this? From the cats and dogs in the streets?

She'd use this Sy with his Renaissance Studies as a rehearsal for the real thing, for Sidney George. Didn't matter how many mistakes she made with him. She'd watch, observe him closely, see what he accepted, what he rejected. He wasn't part of the plan anyway. She had hoped to get directly to the head of the Art Department through Jeff Siegel. They always make it hard for you. Not like the old days.

A Star is Born. She giggled again. This was going to be fun. *Oy*. If Donald ever found out his mother. . . . No, need a different name. What? Sybil Churchill? Hmmm, Sybil Churchill. From *the* Churchills? Bet your ass.

CHAPTER

19

SHE FLOATED DOWN THE CORRIDOR AND KNOCKED ON THE office door. Seymour Rabin. Renaissance Studies. Don't be nervous.

"Hello," she called in. Modulated voice. Very gentile. "I'm Sybil Churchill. So lovely of you to see me."

The rain in Spain falls mainly in the plain. He smiled up at her.

Keep floating, Sybil. Over to the chair at the side of his desk. Glove extended, a touch. "I have a protégé," she plunged right in. "He's moving to Florida and he is such a brilliant artist and critic that he absolutely must be made to teach in one of our schools. He's also very temperamental—you know the type—Michelangelo, Leonardo. I would like to start the process, if I might. Could you give me some . . . clues?"

Sherlock Holmes looked at her. Smiled again. So gracious, these professors. Liked their smiles better than doctor smiles, more real. "It's not difficult. Just talk to Sid, tell him something about the guy, what his credentials are, where he taught last, the shows, you know, things like that."

What schools, what shows? There must be a gallery in California. Who knew the name?

"Will he expect anything else from me?" Ella wondered aloud.

"Well," and Seymour laughed. "You won't have to take him to bed." Ho-ho.

Shmootzik. Your mother should wash out your mouth with

soap talking to a woman my age like this. Dirty pig. She smiled shyly at him. Swallow.

"You have Renaissance. Is the Art Department divided like that too? Do I suggest a period for Donald, for the young man? Is that the way you do it . . . in this school?" Say it that way, leave it open that in Sybil Churchill's university it is done in another way.

"No," Sy added to that. "It will depend on Sid's openings, if indeed there are any, Ms. Churchill." See how they respected you when you were a teacher. Ms., not Mrs., and she didn't look like a feminist either.

"Well, do you think I should enter his domain right now?" Sybil smiled, Sy smiled more radiantly. She hoped her question hadn't sounded foolish. No, he was too dopey to notice. She stood up and bid him adieu. "Ta ta, and have a delightful new year. I do appreciate your time and your courtesy. Bless you."

Ecumenical. Priestly. Sybil Churchill was getting too religious. Cool it.

Little slip of paper tucked into her glove. Directions not too difficult. She soon saw the words Art Department. And the squiggles of color. They probably drew on everything, those fake artists. Sidney George, his sign.

As she was approaching, the door opened, a head popped out. Grayish blond, beard the same, tortoiseshell glasses (as she'd expected) on the nose. "Hello, I'm Sid George. Sy buzzed to say you were on your way up. Wanted to keep you from getting lost."

"No, I'm used to these corridors," she said immediately. "Renaissance is my period and these halls are out of that time." What the hell did she mean by that?

Vague scenes assailed her. When Donald was immersed in his studies, Ella had gone through his books. A good thing for a mother to know a little about what the children were doing, then you could sit down and discuss together. She remembered a few of the names. Botticelli, Raphael. Oh, yes,

Rubens and Titian. No, those two don't sound Italian. She'd concentrate on the Italians, maybe he'd throw in a few.

"My name is Sybil Churchill. I have given up teaching for the nonce, may do it again but in a private school situation." Accepting that? Seemed to. Onward.

"I met a wonderful young man recently. His name is Donald Sager and he's from California. Northern California, naturally. Not the type for the southern part of the state." She winked at good old Sid.

"Really remarkable talent, I must repeat. Well, he has moved to Florida, I've been told. Liked our oranges better, I expect." Waited for him to laugh. He tittered.

"In a university this size you must have openings. This young man would be a definite asset to you. You could use someone like him, Sidney, I'm sure." Couldn't remember which was his first, which the last name. George Sidney, Sidney George.

"I don't want you to think of me as a meddler. No, dear Sidney, think of me as a broker instead, here to arrange a merger. Between you and your department and this bright young man. Do you have any applications I could see?"

"Wait." He laughed. "It takes considerable thinking on my part to determine who gets asked to join this department."

"As well it should, Sidney dear, as well it should. You have to be very careful who comes in, it's your reputation at stake, right?"

That was sinking in, she could see that go down.

"This man, this Sager fellow, has quite a following. Knows important people." Who, who? Sybil, think. "Hilton Kramer, John Canaday, Andy Warhol." (Donald once met him on the corner of Sixteenth Street near Brownie's Restaurant. Warhol dropped an envelope, Donald picked it up.) "Parke Bernet, knew Jackson Pollack. A lot of people. I was terribly impressed by his credentials."

"You saw his credentials? You have his teaching credits?"

"Well, not exactly, which is why I wanted to steal an application blank from you. Just a small one," she pleaded. "Let me take a look and see what information you need."

She went on. "You see, this is a labor of love. I found a lot of good jobs for people over the years. It always worked out well. Sometimes terrific. I swear on the head of Savonarola." Well, he looked amazed at that. She really pulled the name out of the hat. Thank God she traveled after Phil died. Too, Donald had explained paintings to her. Brought her those big magazine-size books of art reproductions that he found on the newsstands in Italy. Talked about brush strokes, about meanings. It was fun. How to explain that to this little bastard?

"Ms. Churchill, I'd have to be convinced he could benefit the school and, mainly, my students."

"Naturally, Mr. George, I don't expect you to take my word for his genius. Why should you? Who am I but another lover of Simonetta Vespucci?" Ella indicated a print on his wall. She had the same one. Piero di Cosimo was the painter. Too bad she hadn't dropped *that* name!

"What would you want to know about Mr. Sager?"

"His background, his teaching credentials, his shows, if any, his available hours. We give teaching fellowships to very talented young men. How old is he?"

"Young."

"Have a glass of sherry, Ms. Churchill." Before she could say no, he poured it.

Sybil Churchill peeled off her gloves. Somewhat like Bubbles LaDome at the local strip joint. It wasn't easy to do. She took large gulps. She was thirsty.

"I'm an open man, Ms. Churchill, and I welcome new talent here. It benefits all of us in the long run, don't you think?"

"*Oui.*" Threw the French word in for class.

"You're a grande dame, Ms. Churchill," he bowed to her.

"*Santé.*" She lifted her glass slightly. He took that to mean encore and refilled it to the top.

"You know, this man could be like the Michelangelo of Florida. Maybe if you hired him for the university he'd paint you a ceiling that would be the talk of this whole country. Personally, I think he could do it. Give him a few students as helpers, a couple of scaffolds. You'd be famous, because you, Sidney dear, would be the patron of the arts."

God, she felt noble. Sybil Churchill was an incredible woman. "I'd even be willing to come in myself and teach a course free, gratis. It would be an honor."

"How could I ask that of you, Ms. Churchill? It's not fair." But he weighed it. "Do you have slides of his work? We don't use applications." That took her by surprise. She had old movies of Marcia and Donnie when they were kids. Phil took them. Maybe a few of Donald at his easel also, painting. She couldn't, however, think of any slides.

"I'm sure Donald has the slides. I've seen them, naturally, and they are very . . . powerful, well-related, aesthetically interesting."

Really clicking there, Sidney being impressed. Thoughtful.

"Ms. Churchill, quite honestly, there is one opening for next fall. If Donald is qualified, I'll talk to him."

Next *fall*? *Gevalt*. Two weeks, she had, to get him out of the house.

"Take this information home with you, Ms. Churchill, and a copy of the catalogue. Our Art Department courses are described here and I'll circle the ones which will be open. Why don't you leave me your phone number so I can reach you? If he's interested, he can write or phone me."

Without thinking, Ella wrote down the correct number. "I have a niece staying with me now and she's a little deaf. Just ask for the old lady or something and don't take no for an answer. My sister's child. Very strange. But I must be patient with her."

"Let me put this in a manila folder for you, Ms. Churchill."

"You are a very nice man, Mr. George. I wish the head of my department had been as nice, I'd still be there."

"Where did you say you taught, Ms. Churchill?"

"Vassar." Why not? If Marcia had better grades, she would have sent her there. Poughkeepsie wasn't a great town, but what a school for a Jewish girl!

"Well." Sidney George got out of his chair for that one. Really hit you in the kishkas, hey, old Sid? She was leaving just in time. The sherry was getting to her.

"I could have danced all night." She smiled.

"What was that?" he inquired.

"Oh, that's my shuffle off to Buffalo number. Leave them in the aisles, you know."

Mr. George had an odd expression on his face. His beard seemed to quiver. Ella or Sybil or whoever the fuck she was felt fine. She closed the door behind her.

"Bullshit" she said to the Renaissance walls. "Bull SHIT!"

CHAPTER

20

Chip was waiting in the car. "How did it go?"

"First of all you don't need a real application. He has to write a letter with his credentials, maybe send some slides, mostly call for an appointment."

"Ella, can you get him to do that?" No more Sybil, goodbye to all that.

"Chip, I have to try. *Oy,* I drank too much sherry too fast. My head hurts. He has to talk to Sidney George, the head of the department."

"Ella, that's not what I asked you. I asked if Donald would make the appointment."

"The answer is no. I'll have to figure some way to set it up myself. Then you can get him there."

". . . . Me?" Why not you, Ella thought. You're going to be the father. She decided not to mention that the opening wouldn't occur until the fall.

"Did he get the art supplies? Do I owe you any money?"

"Don't be silly. Anyway, he started an account in your name. They let him do it because you're in the phone book, lucky you." Chip grinned. "It's a good investment. He'll have the materials, maybe he'll paint."

"Chip, I hate to do this to you, but I'd like to stop and get something for New Year's. Can you just drop me and go on your own way?"

"I wouldn't mind seeing what you get anyway. I'll pretend I'm the sugar daddy."

They were walking around better dresses when Ella spotted the familiar face. "Lois Katz, remember me?"

"Oh, sure, hi, from the group the other day. How's your daughter?"

"Actually, Lois, I'm trying to get her to give you a call. Does it work a little like Alcoholics Anonymous? When you're in trouble over a man, do you call? See, there's someone here in Florida now. Tony Dappolita. . . ."

Lois looked puzzled. "You sure Marcia wants you to tell me this?"

"Oh, yes, I know she would. The truth is, he's trying to use Marcia. You know, like a sex object. And Marcia has no friends her own age here to talk to."

"I couldn't help her much there, Ms. Sagersdorf. I haven't had a man in so long, even my *advice* would be rusty." Chip wandered over to a vacant chair. He needed to sit down for that one.

Lois was going on. "But, say, a sudden thought. Do you know what you would enjoy? And Marcia, too, it's on this very subject. A woman named Andrea Dworkin is speaking on sexuality at the NOW meeting here. Most of the women are younger, college age, but she's a great speaker. I've heard her before. She'll rock you off your chair. If Charlotte Baum opened your head, Andrea will finish the job."

"I don't know. When is it?"

"Tomorrow at eight, I'll write down the address for you. Or look, Geraldine is going and she knows where you live. Why don't you have her pick you up? And Marcia too?"

Ella was considering it. She didn't want her own head opened any more, but it might be good for Marcia. And she knew Marcia would never call Geraldine on her own.

Lois was about to run off, but Ella stopped her. "By the way, my son is here visiting. He's separated from his family." Why did she bother telling her this? She really wanted Donald and Holly to get together again. But maybe he could use some affection, and from what Lois said before, she certainly could use some too.

"Why you sly fox, you." Lois grinned at her. "You have my number, you want to give it to him, go ahead."

Would Donald like this woman? Was she setting this up so they would have a lust and he would move in there? No, no, it was altruism, pure and simple. Lois was lonely, and surely Donald must be getting damn lonely too. Especially in Bimini Towers. It would be her Christmas gift to both of them. And Holly didn't have to know. She'd make Donald swear on a stack of Bibles he'd never say a word to Holly when they got back together. Maybe she'd make it Marcia who happened to introduce Lois.

"I have an idea, Lois. If I invited you for coffee and cake, or even dinner, would you come? Do you have a hard time getting baby sitters?"

"No, it would be a nice thing to do. I'd like it. I don't go to that kind of evening much, and frankly, I miss it."

"After the New Year. Okay? Let's do it right after the first. I'll call."

"Ciao." Lois waved and went off.

Well, two birds with one stone. Lois could become Marcia's friend and Donald's lover. Boy, had she changed. Imagine Ella Sagersdorf arranging a lover for her son. Oh, there were days way back then when she arranged for Donald to meet the niece of this doctor, the daughter of that manufacturer. Those were for marriage, never for sleeping together. Ella hoped all the girls from those days were virgins. They'd been promised intact and she trusted the packagers. She remembered the buildups she used to give. The one had blond hair, that one had a good personality, the other was peppy. What did she say to prepare him for Lois? She's cute, she's divorced? She's great in bed? She thrashes around a lot? Maybe she didn't even like to go to bed with men anymore. Maybe her marriage was so bad, her husband so terrible, worse even than Stanley the worm, that she'd given up sex forever. But her Donald was a charmer. He'd melt that girl. She'd look at those green eyes, she'd go limp. He was so slim, he seemed to have a big bundle in his jockey shorts (tee hee). A mitzvah. She'd introduce Gable to Lombard. They'd pant for each other.

And Marcia? Marcia would hate it. Her friend Lois going to bed with her brother Donald. Fire and brimstone. Ella would have to find a subtle way to handle this. No fighting. A love-in.

"I thought you were going to try on some dresses?" Chip had been very patient.

"Now. I'll rush, I promise. Marilyn Monroe I'll be."

She selected a black, a navy, and a very interesting burgundy. She loved that color. That and real purple. When you wore either of them, you felt like a different woman. She hoped the burgundy would look better than the blue or the black. Those two were sensible colors, better buys, but Ella was not a sensible dresser. She dressed by whim. Tried to hide the extra weight in the best way a manufacturer knew how, but hoped the color would knock out the beholder so he'd never notice the girth. Put the black on first. Went out to the floor to find Chip. He nodded at her, nice. Smiling. Walked up to him with the tag. It's eighty dollars. Let me show you one of the others. It's a real bargain. Reduced from one hundred and ten to seventy. Imagine.

She rushed back inside. The burgundy had long sleeves and a flattering neckline. Good for her. She still had a slim neck and, thank God, few wrinkles so she could get away with showing it. This dress would look wonderful with the garnet necklace she bought in Florence. Leah thought she was crazy. It's the kind of thing your husband gets for you, what woman walks around buying herself expensive jewelry? Me, thought Ella. And bought the garnet earrings to match.

She knew it looked good. Could see Chip's expression

change from nice to perfect. She wouldn't even have to bother with the navy one, just give it back to the salesgirl.

"Ella, you look like a movie star."

"Isn't it a bargain? Can you believe this tag?" and she pulled it close to Chip's face.

"Ella, don't yell at me, but I want to buy it for you. And I know you're going to make a fuss. But I insist. While you're here, buy the wedding dress and pay for that yourself. That pleasure I leave you." A prince of a man.

"Well, I'll tell them to put this in a box, sweetheart, and you take it to the car. I want the wedding dress to be a surprise."

She turned back to the racks. There's one with a jabot. Loved jabots, nice little ruffles at the throat. Make her look like a sixty-five-year-old virgin. Selected a peach dress also, realizing it was the same color as Ida's New Year's outfit. Tried them both on in the dressing room. Went outside in the peach to find Esperanza. Jewish saleswomen were a little too conservative for Ella. Esperanza, a Cuban exile, had more of Ella's kind of pizzazz.

"Esperanza." She found the frizzled redhead bending over the adjustments desk. "Come and tell me what you think of my wedding dress."

"Missus Esageresdoff, you are marrying that nice mans? I'm esso happy for you." She hugged Ella.

"Tell me the truth. I'll waltz around a little in this one."

"I don have to essee the other. This is the perfeck color for a bride. Perfeck. You put on pearls here around the neck, esso, and little earrings, and perfeck. Listen to me."

"I feel the same way. Just wanted your opinion. Will you write it up for me? Here's my credit card."

She'd have to change that come January. No more Ella Sagersdorf. Now Mrs. Hyman Leon Lowe. Ella Lowe. She'd better start practicing the signature. She'd been Sagersdorf for so many years, it was hard to think of any other name.

Mrs. Hyman Lowe. Hy Lowe. Hey. She giggled. No wonder he called himself Chip. Not once in these months had it occurred to her. What's in a name? Melanie Flumenhoff. Tooraloora Epstein. Kilo Watts.

Laugh too hard, her mother used to tell her, and you'll cry. Get into the car with Chip, drive home to Bimini Towers, and you'll see what's to laugh about.

CHAPTER

21

SHE COULD HEAR THE SHOUTING AS THEY WALKED DOWN THE hall to her apartment. Worry about Ida Alpert hearing? The entire tenth floor was witness.

She hurried her steps to interrupt. Maybe Donald hadn't honed his language yet.

"You stupid cunt!" Obviously far too late.

"Chip, I'll ring the bell, maybe they'll stop."

The door was jerked open. "Oh, hi, Ella dear, come in." Her son bowed. Bad sign. Practically shoved the door into Chip's face.

"Chip's here too." A warning to them both. The way she used to do it on West End Avenue. If you don't watch out . . . hmmm, what? No allowance? Maybe not a bad idea still.

Donald whirled into the bedroom and slammed that door next.

Leaving a red-eyed princess. "Ma, I can't be left alone with him. He just won't give me a second's peace. Am I supposed to know the lives of every painter, every book ever written? I know other things. He won't believe it."

Donald had counted to ten. He came out of the room, crossed to the kitchen. She could hear the ice cubes.

"That's all you hear from him, ice cubes clinking into glasses." Marcia was right. It was a sound she associated with Donald.

He came back with the ice and plenty of vodka to cover it. "Chip, you want something to drink?"

"No," Chip answered. "I have another suggestion. Why don't the three of you come out with me for a change?"

"Good idea," Ella leaped to reply. Before they had a chance to realize they were each other's date. "Go, both of you, and get ready, and Chip and I will decide where to go. A movie, how about a movie?"

"I hate movies," Donald told her. "And I hate most plays." Adding that in case she should have an alternate suggestion.

"Maybe we could find a film you'd *like*, Donald," Chip told him. Donald looked surprised. Another person whose opinion he'd have to consider.

"Can't we come to a majority opinion? Do we have to do what *he* wants?" Marcia spat. "If he doesn't like the movie, he can sit outside in the car and we can get him a bottle of vodka with a nipple on it."

"I don't need to go at all, you know." His last offering.

"Look, I want you both to come," Chip insisted. "Your mother would be happy if it worked out too. Can't you have a truce for this evening?" Bless that man, he really was on her side.

The doorbell rang. Sylvia.

"I tried to get you on the phone, Ella," she started, push-ing into the room. "Hello. Donald, I saw you drawing Ida Alpert by the pool. You draw well. Very flattering. My daugh-ter always said she'd like a painting of me. Do you think you'd like to do it? I'd pay, of course."

Ella couldn't believe it. Sylvia was asking on her own. With no coaching. Would Donald believe it, though?

"Donald, what do you think?" Sylvia was persisting. "I'd make the time, cancel dates, anything I'd have to do."

"Sylvia, he charges one hundred fifty dollars. And that's a special rate. He gets much more in California." Donald wasn't a good businessman. Ella'd have to set the figure. And tell Ida to keep her mouth shut. For such a bargain, she'd be mum.

"That's fine with me. Donald?" Sylvia turned to him once again.

"I guess so. What's the best time for you?"

"I'm up at six in the morning. Anytime after that would be good."

"I don't see that hour except as the other side of midnight." Donald said. "Make it around ten. Do you have good light in your living room or do you want to come down to the pool?"

"You pick me up and you decide. Tomorrow. Gotta run. . . ."

Sylvia was ready. Ella raced over. For the hug. "Goodbye, Syl. Thanks. And I'll see you tomorrow."

"God bless," Sylvia replied. "I hope you're practicing for the show, Marcia." And she was gone.

"Boy," Ella said, "you're going to have a lot of money in a few days, Donald."

"Yeah, I can go out and get laid," he snorted. "For cash."

"Don't go bringing any prostitutes to this apartment," Ella was quick to caution.

"Ella, do you really think I'd bring a hooker into your sacred palace? Never. Perish the thought."

"You don't have to be so snotty. You're living in this palace, right?"

"Yeah, I'm here. Nowhere else to go or I would have. Do you think I want to spend the rest of my goddamn life like this?"

Did she have to answer him? God forbid, she wanted to say.

"Look, everybody, get ready and let's go. The argument will sound better at a restaurant." Chip was still trying his peacemaking number.

"You're crazy, Chip, to want this family at all," Marcia decided to put in.

Shut up. Who needs you to make that comment? Let him have this family if he wants it.

"I know what's good for me, Marcia. Don't worry."

Of course he knows what's good for him. Think he just came to Miami yesterday? He's met plenty of widows, even a few marrieds who would throw over their shlemiel husbands for this one. Think it was easy for me to find him, to break through the crowd?

Ella loved that first real meeting. Passover. He was invited to the same seder. Outnumbered by women as always in Miami, but it was a pretty small group. She did her impression of *Fiddler on the Roof*, Tevye as the rabbi presiding over the table. Sang the songs afterwards like Jewish rock. Leah sat there and rubbed tears of laughter out of her eyes. Chip was enchanted. Kept coming over to tell her how wonderful she was.

Took a few dates after that, he stopped laughing, started to think of her as a person. They talked quietly. She didn't stop joking; no, that was a part of her. But he found several sides of Ella to love. Some of the other women, well, they weren't too complex. Lots of them were desperate. They didn't like to live alone. They didn't know what it meant, not to be a servant, not to have a master. Like little dogs, lost. Waiting for someone to come along and order them to do this, do that. Phil, rest his soul, never came on like that. She didn't think she would have liked it, if he had. There were things the husband wasn't expected to do and the wife's day in the home was such a busy one. That's why they look for a new man to nurse. They complain about the loneliness. Especially bad after five o'clock. They would band together around the dinner hour, keeping one another company, raising spirits. But finally, after dinner, after all the talk, you had to come back. To your own apartment, walk in, lock the door. A lamp would be on, at least one, everybody burned a lamp. And then the quiet. Go from room to room, fluffing a pillow, running a finger along surfaces. Everything so clean, who would dirty it?

The television set, that was company. Voices talked at you, a face familiar every evening. So you went into the bathroom,

removed your clothes, put a net around your hair. Some
women, Ella knew, took off a wig, exposed their few fine gray
strands to the night air. You pulled down the spread, sipped
a little glass of brandy to help you sleep, maybe a Valium for
some, a sleeping pill for the ones whose doctors prescribed it,
and lay back to watch. The sitcoms, Merv Griffin, the news
people, Johnny Carson. Friends, these were. And meet their
friends, the celebrities. Getting more tired, the Valium, the
brandy, the sleeping pill working. Once more to the toilet.
Under the covers. Almost asleep. So tired, try not to think,
try not to worry, try not to remember loss. During the day
you'll have real company. Sleep so you can wake up and get
out of here.

Ella must have dozed in the chair. Too much of that sherry
this afternoon, not used to it. Donald was reading the news-
paper in the dining area, Chip she could see standing near the
radio in the kitchen. But Marcia seemed to be missing.

"Where is everybody? Why are you keeping me waiting?"

"Ma, you were sleeping." Marcia after all, out of the bedroom. And a change of clothes, even. "Come on, we're ready."

Looking good, her Marcia, an actual improvement since
she arrived. And Donald folding his paper like a mensch now
also?

"So. Up, up, everybody. Chip, the *kinder* are ready, the
mommy is set."

The All-American family is going out on the town.

CHAPTER

22

SURPRISING HOW SHE MANAGED TO LIVE THROUGH YET AN-
other day. Walked through the apartment now, dusting, pok-
ing, trying to create order.

Marcia was practicing on the violin. It sounded pleasant
and was calming Ella.

"What are you going to play, 'Love in Bloom'?" Donald
threw the question at Marcia.

"Look, Donald, I can probably play the violin better than
you can paint. Did you ever think of that?"

"Shut up, both of you. We spent maybe one hour together
today, is that too much? I left sandwiches, the elves ate
them. I made a buffet supper, you shouldn't have to look at
each other." Frankly, Ella was fed up. If she were a magician,
she'd make them disappear in a cloud of smoke. Her luck,
the memory would linger on.

"Donald, we're being picked up in five, ten minutes. I told
you we're going out?"

"I'm sitting on tenterhooks, waiting. How come you didn't
insist I come along?"

"Men aren't invited, my dear brother. This is for women
only."

"Maybe I could sneak in wearing one of your wigs."

"I don't wear wigs, you creep. And they'd throw you out.
You smell like a pig in addition to acting like one."

"Okay!" Ella screamed this time. "Meshuggeners. Enough.
I live here and I can't stand this kind of noise. I'm putting
on the phonograph this minute." She shuffled through the

records to find one loud enough and dramatic enough to drown them out. Beethoven's Ninth. Perfect. She had the Toscanini set.

"It will be playing when we leave, Donald. Don't forget to turn off the power before you go out."

She realized she had no idea where he was going. Did he have any cash at all?

"Donald, come here, I want to show you something about the phonograph."

"Ella, I know how to turn off the damn machine."

"Your mother is the boss and she is saying come here. C-o-m-e h-e-r-e."

He came. She slipped a twenty-dollar bill into his hand as she described the power mechanism.

He kissed her cheek and squeezed the hand that fed him. "I'll take the other key, since you and Marcia will be out together, okay?"

She agreed. "You don't have to wait for us to leave, Donald, if you want to go now." Get him to leave, let her have three moments of peace before Geraldine buzzed for them to come down.

The buzzer instead. "Marcia, she's here already. Let's go. Donald, lock the door, don't forget. Double lock, Donald."

He waved her off. He never forgot things like that, why did she worry anyway? He was as obsessively neat as she was.

"What kind of evening will this be?" Ella asked as she folded herself into the back of Geraldine's car. Another woman sat in the front. She patted the seat next to her for Marcia. Her own mother used to pat seats this way. What was the purpose? Warm it up for her tushie?

"Hello." An Afro hairdo turned their way from the front. "I'm Carole Cavalcanti."

"What an interesting name," Ella heard herself say. "It's Italian, right?"

"On my father's side, Jewish on my mother's." She shook Marcia's hand. "I'll answer your question about the evening if you want. I've heard Andrea Dworkin speak before."

Women speaking by themselves. Not squeezed into a sandwich between six men on a talk show. Good things must be happening. Not too many of those evenings when Ella was young. Panels of women, you could be sure the subject was New Recipes or Thirty Ways to Decorate Your Home. Now, the subject was sexuality.

"Carole, what will she talk about in sexuality? What does it mean? How to do it?" Ella hated to admit her confusion, but she wanted to be prepared before she walked in.

"No, Ms. Sagersdorf. Andrea is a radical feminist and she'll be talking about philosophy and morality and ethics, not how to do it. Maybe why *not*, sometimes." Carole laughed.

"I'm prepared for enlightenment," Ella stated. She wanted them to know, to tell their friends that Marcia's mother was one of the . . . not girls, one of the women.

They walked into an auditorium which was very full. A lot of young women. A lot of blue jeans, overalls, T-shirts. Not very much makeup, and Ella shifted uncomfortably. She had had sense enough to wear pants, plain gray ones, but they weren't blue jeans. Marcia was wearing jeans. A year ago, Ella would have called it a jeans outfit. Now it was a uniform. Ella was wearing a blouse and the plainest sweater she owned. Not a bead on it. Somehow she had known that beads were a no-no.

Good-looking and bright-faced young women—most of them probably Pamela's age. She could imagine her granddaughter in an audience such as this. Lois was waving at them. "I saved seats for you all, slide in."

Ella slid. She was farthest over and smiled at the very young girl on her right. So clean she was, all in white. They lied, people who said this generation was dirty. She never saw dirty ones down here. They wore their hair long, boys and girls, but always clean. Definitely clean.

She looked toward the stage. There were several women up there. One she recognized from the meeting at Lois's house.

The taller one in the middle she supposed was Andrea Dworkin. She must be the radical feminist. She rolled the words around on her tongue. Radical feminist. Andrea looked like such a strong girl. A solid girl. With a nice face. Ella wondered what her mother was like. Whether she was here tonight. If she were the mother, she would go along. She'd be so proud of Marcia, she'd walk around with a button saying *I'm the Mother.*

Ella realized that it was quite a crowd. How did things like this go on around town and never enter her circle? She had lived here for several years and it took a crisis visit from Marcia to open up such worlds for her.

A woman came to the microphone and introduced the subject and brought the speaker to the front. Andrea began. My, she had a good strong voice too. Ella leaned forward. She was using some bad language, but Ella didn't blush at all. And the voice never faltered. She had a hypnotic effect, Ella saw the whole audience lean forward. It was hard to absorb all the things she was saying. Ella never thought you had so many choices. This woman insisted you not only had choices but that you had to fight for the right to be and do what you wanted. She said we are raped every day. Raped? Society? The ideas were fighting themselves within her. When you're my age, Ella thought, it is hard to throw out the garbage and be completely clean with new thoughts. Well, she could listen. This person was a good arguer, she should go into politics. Ella knew she'd vote for Andrea Dworkin. If she were back in New York, she'd nominate Bella Abzug for every office so she could vote for her too. They had something in common, Bella and this Andrea. Said things that were hard to accept. But if you listened, they began to make sense. *Oy,* she was saying more about men and women. And the way they related sexually. Ella blushed because she knew what Andrea said was true. Self-evident. That's the word. A person like this gets up, says things you don't think about all the time and—she thought—why do I feel like crying?

She'd like to invite Andrea to dinner. Maybe she could talk some sense into Marcia. Donald? Oh, he would hate her. Such a threat she would be to him. *She*'d tell him where to jam it.

Maybe when Leah comes home from the cruise, after New Year's, she'd arrange a dinner. Imagine, this Andrea and Charlotte, and Leah and herself. The Jewish women in America. She smiled at the thought. As the applause engulfed her, she shut her eyes.

It would have to be casual. She'd explain to Leah. These young women wouldn't want a formal meal with candlesticks and things like that. She'd get some mats, that's right, some tatami mats and put them on the floor. She'd push the table against the wall and use it as a buffet, show them how simple she could be. Just because she was an older person didn't mean she was a typical Jewish mother. Holly had sent Ella a caftan from Morocco, she'd wear that.

"Hello, Charlotte and Andrea. Come in, this is my friend Leah, also a feminist." Charlotte is wearing the same long skirt from the Sisterhood meeting and that nice, thick hair is loose. Andrea is in overalls with a T-shirt and wearing simple jewelry. Clean, both of them, very clean. They couldn't be cleaner if they were bathed by Sylvia Perlmutter herself.

"The food is all ready so we don't have to go into the kitchen and prepare it." Did feminists help each other in the kitchen? Did they all work together so nobody was the slave? Well, probably. That's why Ella had everything ready, to avoid four bodies clashing in that small kitchen. They'd fill their plates with the health food she'd fixed and sit around.

"Let's talk about Jewish mothers and Jewish daughters," Leah would open. And Jewish sons, Ella meant to add.

"We'd be happy to," they said in unison.

"Why didn't our mothers tell us these wonderful new things when we were young girls?" Leah might ask.

Charlotte answered that one. "They told you different things. Maybe about voting, or striking for better wages."

Leah replied to her. "Actually, they told us to look for a

guy, hold on, work like a horse, and take care of him until he dies."

"Life doesn't need to have such a narrow scope," Andrea said.

"Have a piece of fruit," Ella extended the bowl.

"You have a granddaughter, Ella?" This from Charlotte.

"I have three."

"Some of them will choose not to get married at all." She couldn't believe Charlotte was right. "I have two daughters and if they make that decision, I wouldn't be shocked."

"I probably would be," Leah persisted. "If my granddaughters don't marry, I would be shocked. Or if they became, you know, lesbians."

"That isn't the end of the world, women loving women," Andrea said gently. "They could be both."

Ella got up and came back with a tray. "Have a piece of cake."

"Did it ever occur to you, Leah, that one of your granddaughters might be president of the United States?" Charlotte asked.

Leah shook her head. It hadn't occurred to Ella either, but why admit it when you're not directly questioned?

"A woman president? How about a Jewish president?" Ella inquired. "Which will happen first?"

"How about Bella Abzug, she'd be both." Leah echoed her own feelings.

"Maybe you could start a new political party," Andrea suggested.

"I'd like to," Leah said.

Ella could vouch for that. Leah was in every reform movement that came along. Reform Democrats, reform Republicans, reform Jews, reformed prisoners, reform social security, reform welfare, reformed Jesus freaks. They found Leah a willing advocate.

"We do need to elect women candidates. On a national scale," Charlotte said.

Ella agreed. She would check to make sure she didn't get one of those crazy anti-abortion women, but otherwise, she would cast her ballot for the women candidates.

"Have either of you ever thought of running for Congress down here?" Andrea looked at both of them.

"Have another piece of fruit?" Ella offered.

"If you would run, Ella, I'd work for you," Leah said firmly.

"I'm sure you would, Leah, but how would I know what to do once I got elected?"

Charlotte spoke up at once. "What makes you think that an intelligent Jewish woman like yourself couldn't run the government better than it has been run in the past?"

She couldn't answer that question. Andrea was already forming her own answer.

"Look, women like you have to take firm action. You can't expect your granddaughters to do it alone."

"Do you think it's possible that Ella and I could run a campaign here in Florida? There's enough women to vote and outnumber the men, I'll tell you that."

"Anyone want another piece of cake?"

"Did you mention that you had brothers, Ella?" Andrea was so gentle for a radical person.

"Yes, I did."

"Did they have careers?" she asked again.

"All of them," Ella answered honestly. "I'm the only girl in the family. And the only one who didn't have a career. My parents didn't think it was important."

"How about your own daughter? Were you different with her?" That Andrea could really get to you.

"No, only Donald. I sent Marcia to college to get a good husband."

"Are you happy with what she got?" Charlotte now asked.

Leah and Ella tittered together: "Stanley the worm."

Ella had to admit, "I did a bad job with her."

"Well, you see, Ella," Charlotte summed up, "there are

very subtle things a mother can do, or not do, to totally mold or mess up her daughter's life."

Leah took up the standard. "Ella and I are so impressed with you. You've changed our thinking. We will probably reform ourselves immediately and change the world in which we live."

Ella was so astounded by Leah's speech that she opened her eyes.

A young woman was addressing a question to Andrea Dworkin. The woman in front of Ella was crying. Crying. She noticed that several of the young women were crying also. How did Andrea manage to do this? In plays, yes, she'd seen an actress do this, but with just words in a speech, how?

She glanced at Marcia, sitting between Carole and Lois. She looked very pale, very intense. You got an earful, huh? she thought.

Applause again, and the meeting was closed. "We're going to have some coffee together," Lois said. "Will you and Marcia join us?"

"Good," she answered, "but first I want to say something to Andrea."

She walked toward the stage. Andrea was coming down the staircase. Friends seemed to be waiting.

"Darling, I just wanted to tell you how much I enjoyed your talk. Your mother must be so proud of you."

"I hope she is," Andrea responded. "Some of the things I say aren't easy for a mother to accept."

"I accept, she'll accept. Trust me," Ella said.

CHAPTER

23

THEY CHOSE THE COFFEE SHOP OF THE DORAL. IT WAS NOT a well-lit place and Ella wasn't too happy with it. It's not the kind of place she and her older set of friends would have visited.

They were seated at a round table, all eight of them. The conversation was very animated. Even Marcia was taking part.

Ella looked around the room, wondering if anyone she knew was there. To see her with this remarkable group of women. She peered through the dimness. Someone who looked like Rabbi Waldman and his wife with a couple, hopefully from the temple. To the right of them a familiar face. Who?

Oh, my God, no. Let it not be. She stared harder. *Oy.* It was, it was Donald. Drunk, she could tell he was drunk. The way he held up his head with his hands. Who was he with? Whoever she was, she had the bosom of a Playboy bunny, Ella could see that from here. Even in this light. She looked over at Marcia, deep in conversation. Protect her, dear God, make her blind for the next hour. How do you come from a radical feminist meeting to see your older brother sitting with a Playboy bunny?

"Girls, my rabbi is sitting on the other side, I'm just going to say hello." They continued to chatter. She got up to walk in that direction, keeping her face averted so Donald wouldn't have a chance to see her approach. Catch him by surprise, that's the best way.

She neared the table. In time to see the Playboy bunny's

tongue leave the pure kosher ear of her firstborn. "What a surprise! Donald dear, I was on my way to say hello to a friend."

"What the hell, you following me?" He giggled. "Hey, Ma. Ella. This is Maureen O'Hara. Say hello."

"Hello, dear." This didn't look like the real Maureen O'Hara. With the flaming red hair, the green eyes, the fine bones, a nice girl *that* Maureen. This Maureen had been on covers of magazines. Sticking those big boobs in people's faces, she'd bet, and don't ask what else she's showing.

"You son's a gas, a real trip, Mrs. Sager. Are we having a time. Wow."

Temple Art School. A master's degree from Indiana. A teaching fellow in Cambridge. He needed to wind up in the coffee shop of the Doral . . . drunk with a piece of cheesecake on his lap. Maureen O'God forbid. She should turn to the next table, introduce him there. Rabbi, I want you to meet my son the artist, the connoisseur of beauty. Doesn't he have fine taste, look at this Botticelli he's got tonight. Botticelli indeed.

"I'm just having some coffee with my friends from the women's group. Don't bother to get up."

Maureen looked puzzled. "You sing, or play, in this group?"

"It's not that kind of group, dear. It's a political group. You know, the kind that takes over the world."

Donald huffed. "Ella, don't wait up for me. Maureen is drying me out a bit before she puts me back into the fresh air again. Our evening is just beginning. . . ."

Does this hooker know he only has twenty bucks? She would put him in the fresh air immediately if she knew.

"I have to go to the little girl's room. Be right back," Maureen sang.

"You have enough money?" Such a first question, she asked him.

"Can you slip me another twenty? It will be well spent, believe me, Ella. See how I'm enjoying myself."

Shmuck. She passed him the bill. "Don't embarrass me in front of my friends. There's a couple of people I want you to meet when you're not so drunk. Is that Maureen a real person? —you know what I mean."

"Of course, she's real, Ella. Didn't you see those tits?"

"That's not what I mean, Donald. You know very well what I mean. Is she, you know?"

"No, she's not. She's a nice girl, a dancer. Between shows and husbands. That's why she needs me."

"Don't get fresh with me, Donald. Show some respect. The rabbi is right near us." Knew as she was saying it that it was a mistake.

It was. Out it tumbled. He did it all the time, the *boruch*, the whole bar mitzvah prayer. She turned her back to the rabbi's table, maybe they won't recognize the sweater, put her eyes to the ceiling and waited for it to be over.

And did he have to do it so loud? Everybody was looking, some, rather most of them, smiling.

What's to smile? A drunk man in his forties reciting his bar mitzvah, that's funny? He finished. Thank God Maureen O'Hara was still peeing, didn't have to sit through this to repeat to her *Irisher* friends.

"Look, Donald, I'm going now. Try to remember you're a good boy. And that I love you. Have some dignity."

Maureen O'Hara waved at her, coming back from the bathroom, three ounces of Elizabeth Arden's Blue Grass perfume announcing her arrival.

No one at her own table had noticed a thing, conversation was still animated. "The rabbi is so much fun," Ella announced merrily.

CHAPTER

24

"ELLA, YOU HAVE TO TELL THEM WE'RE GETTING MARRIED. It's not a sin, you know." Chip was disturbed, she could tell.

"Look, they know we go together, what difference will it make if they don't know yet? I'm paving the way, they shouldn't feel guilty. I'm their mother, I know." A line she'd used with Phil.

"I don't understand them," Phil always said, said until the day he dropped dead. Died of a heart attack. No trouble to Ella. One minute there, the next not. No hospital bills, no private nurses. Clean and considerate. The way he'd been in life.

"Ella, you know them, I don't," Phil kept insisting. "Just let me know what decisions you make so I don't look like a dope."

She didn't expect him to understand them. So how could she explain them to Chip?

"Chip, tonight is New Year's. They're both coming. We'll all be in a good mood, we can talk about it then. Marcia is getting into women's liberation. She likes those peope, who knows what will happen? Donald's got money coming from the portraits. I looked at the one he's started of Sylvia. He's making her look good. Don't worry, he'll have dozens, twenty more, begging him to paint. I'll talk to him about the teaching job. It will all work out. Don't worry. Chip, please?"

So how come *she* was worried? Couldn't wait for Leah to get home the day after New Year's. Leah could cope with those two. Bossed them around a lot, but they listened to her.

Maybe she would have a plan. Leah always had plans. Tell her hello and that she had fourteen days to change Ella's life.

"You know, we didn't talk about a honeymoon, did we? Chip, what do you think?"

If they took a honeymoon, she'd have an extra two weeks. Put Leah in charge. If they're not out by the wedding day, give them a reprieve through the honeymoon. Then, out. O-U-T. D-Day.

"You know, you're absolutely right. I should think about it. There's one thing I've always wanted to do more than anything in my life, and that's travel in Israel. Do you think we could get passports and reservations and get moving by then?"

"Chip, I can't think of anything more exciting. But can you do it so fast?"

"Ella, I'm going to go to a travel agent I know. If he thinks it can be done, I'll start it moving. Meanwhile why don't you take a nap? Be rested for tonight?"

He was right. She would. Kissed him goodbye. Though there were chores before she could get any sleep.

Donald was next door, putting color to Ida Alpert. Ida was thrilled. Rushed in this morning, dressed to kill in the peach for New Year's, pulling Donald away from his coffee. Only Ella knew how hung over he was. Too much vodka and too much Maureen O'Hara. He'd admitted as much when she cornered him outside the bathroom door.

"Yeah, I got in around three-thirty, four. I'm out of it today."

Good, maybe he'd behave tonight. "And do me a big favor, Donald. Be dignified at the party. And dance with some of the widows."

"Ella, come on. That's asking too much."

"No, it isn't asking anything. You're here. You're a nice Jewish boy, what a thrill you'd give them. Don't be so hard, Donnie. And maybe they'll ask you to do some portraits, the money will be worth a little two-step, a polka, the hustle."

"Ella, you're good enough to hand me money when I need it, to give me a place to sleep, to protect me from my bitch of a sister, how can I fail you now?"

"She is not a bitch. If you gave her a chance, you'd see what a nice person she is. . . ."

"What's your preference, a son who dances with your widow friends or a brother who talks nice to his sister and stays home on New Year's Eve?"

"Be a bastard for a while longer. I do need you to circulate around the dance floor. It is really going to be beautiful, Donnie."

The Decorations Committee had been fixing up since yesterday. Crepe paper, balloons, she could see them from the lobby. The big ballroom was a perfect place with tables the way they'd planned it. More like a theater or a cabaret. Too depressing to have couples at tables and all the single women alone together.

She was on the Entertainment Committee. Indeed, she was the main event. Had her routines down pat. When her kids were little, they always told her that nobody else's mother did this. Of course not. You think the whole world is full of Jewish comic mothers? She had a feeling they wished she were more like Lily Pons or Grace Moore, an opera star, classy. Trilling the scales, not singing "I'm a red-hot mama, but I'm blue for you. . . ." Her children were repressed, that's their problem. Bounce, bounce, bump, bump, she practiced.

Marcia had two numbers. One Brahms, and a Prokofiev. Add a little class. She'd schedule that right after Shirley Mittelman doing Carmen Miranda. Then Fanny Sussman on the piano, a couple of old tunes, and Ella for the finale. Lenny Feldstein, the orchestra leader, said he would do a few comic shtiks in between the ladies. It ought to go well.

But she missed Leah. First New Year's they hadn't been together. Every year, whatever. Even if she and Phil made other plans, Leah would come over for an hour or so, or she and Phil would have a drink there. Always welcomed in the year together. She hoped Leah would toast her on the high seas.

It would be exciting to take a honeymoon trip with Chip. She remembered her three weeks in London with Phil, staying with Donald and Holly. No kids yet, back in the era of swinging London with the miniskirts and all. Holly looked adorable, those long legs and that blond hair. She and Phil were so happy to be with them. The room they slept in was Donald's study and it was very grand. Big windows looking out over the Thames. Chelsea Embankment. So romantic.

And Holly and Donald were such a compatible couple. So very close, they talked about the same things, really seemed good friends. What could have happened? After all those years together, and now the kids, what was the reason for the split? People used to remark how gorgeous their children would be. And they were, really lovely little girls. Took the best from each of them.

Maybe people needed a rest from each other. Those two spent so much time together. Holly only started her business four years ago, before that they had been inseparable day and night. She wasn't trying to get rid of her husband just because she was successful, Ella was sure of that. It had to go a lot deeper.

Wanted to go to Italy with Phil. Had an itinerary planned when he died. Not one to give up easily, she went to Irving, sobbed her eyes out, made him feel bad, terrible, got him to let Leah go in Phil's place, to take care of Ella in her bereavement. Of course, Ella, of course. No question, he said. She walked slowly from his study, found Leah in the kitchen, whispered he said yes, he said yes. They giggled, clung to each other, dancing around the kitchen, weeping with joy.

Ella put on her sad face for other people. Phil would want her to have a good time. But a widow was not supposed to smile, especially not within a year of her husband's death. She was supposed to mourn properly, "May his soul rest in peace"

as a preface to every sentence, that was the rule. She loved
Phil, she didn't need to announce it. Didn't mean she should
die when he did. She could take care of herself.

"Wear black to the airport, let Irv feel I'm the nurse, don't
forget," Leah warned her. She did, black veil and all. Irving
bade them farewell with tears in his eyes. Praised his wife for
taking care of her friend. Good woman.

They laughed for two whole months, the duration of their
trip. At all the mistakes in language, at the food wrongly
ordered. Ella traveled with an Italian and Spanish Berlitz.
"We will not be typical American tourists, Leah. We'll
memorize as many phrases as we can and try to communicate
with the people in the countries we visit."

They were starting in Italy and ending in Spain. The travel
agent promised them a perfect trip and he was right.

They walked everywhere. In Florence stayed at a little
pensione on the Piazzale Michelangelo side of the Arno. They
sallied forth daily with the Michelin Guide, with other tourist
books, with Vasari's *Lives of the Painters* (Donald's gift to
her), with a book on the Medici, all tucked into Ella's big
black bag. They drank up the city, discussed it endlessly,
speculated about retiring there. "Wouldn't it be great, Leah,
when we're little old ladies, you know, very short, very
stooped, to move here to Italy? To live in a grand apartment
with marble floors and lots of paintings on the walls?"

Leah laughed. "Two little old Jewish ladies shlepping up
to Vatican City to kiss the Pope's tunic."

"Or we could actually live in Rome. Like Vivien Leigh—
what was that movie?"

"The one where she picked up young boys?"

"Well, I don't quite have that in mind, unless you have
other plans, you dirty old lady, you." Ella kissed her on the
cheek.

They both loved the art of Italy and Ella found herself
feeling very close to Donald. Beginning to understand what
he was about, how his head worked.

Had an especially good time in Venice. Stayed at the Danieli, very elegant. Went to Johnny's Bar for a drink, well, the aperitivo she thought of as a drink. Met an American there who owned a small airline. He bought them both drinks, more than she and Leah had taken on the entire trip. They got bubbly, Ella started to perform. Spike, for that was his name, oh, yes, insisted they join him for dinner with two Italian friends. One was an aristocratic Milanese businessman, the other a funny and highly spirited Neapolitan who ran ahead to order the pasta, the pasta perfecta. Dinner was indeed that and she and Leah were danced around the floor. How she wished then she were about thirty, forty at the most. How wonderful life would be, so much ahead of her, so much excitement.

She and Leah still whispered about that evening in Venice. Spike took them for a gondola ride afterwards as if to ensure that this would be a most memorable night. She couldn't think of Italy without thinking of Venice and of Venice without remembering Spike Wellington and Peppino the Neapolitan and Paolo the Milanese. They had become major personages in her life. It seemed a downhill path since. Until Chip. Then it changed.

Look at her. She's dreaming when she should be sleeping. She wanted to be in tip-top shape. Really in the best of form. She had two extra guests. Two little cherubim singing Happy New Year. And to all a good night.

CHAPTER

25

ELLA WAS GETTING APPREHENSIVE. WHY DOES HE HAVE TO drink so much? She looked over to the bar. Donald was planted there, young sapling waiting to grow roots. That patroness of the arts, Ida Alpert, had stationed herself beside him. One little favor, Ella'd asked him for. Dance with a couple of my friends, please. And given him a list. Made up a fun dance card. Put at the top, Donnie Sager, His Night. Waited for the smile. None. Should have sensed the signals, felt the bad vibrations. Didn't.

Early in the evening he had waltzed Sylvia Perlmutter. She was the only exception Ella allowed. The rest should be widows.

Perhaps she had made a larger mistake. Look at his condition and not yet eleven o'clock. Not showtime. And she had phoned Lois Katz.

"Lois, darling, what plans do you have for New Year's?"

"Really smashing ones, Ella. The kids and I watch TV. At midnight I open a can of smoked oysters and a split of champagne. We eat the oysters on crackers, guzzle the champagne, and go to bed."

"Look, dear, do you think you could leave them alone for a couple of hours and come see the show at Bimini Towers? I'm in it, and Marcia is doing a couple of solos on the violin." No mention of Donald, not a whisper.

"That sounds like an offbeat number. Maybe I can get my

niece to take my place with the oysters and the champagne. How much is the cover charge?"

"Don't get me upset. You'll be our guest. I won't hear of anything else."

Set. She was coming. To meet Prince Charming. That lush at the bar. She decided to risk a walk over there.

"Ida, darling, you look beautiful."

"Ella, darling, so do you," her son responded. "Star of stage, screen, and radio, what are you planning for tonight—cancer?" He had the nerve to laugh at that.

"Ida, my son has a warped sense of values. That, he calls humor. How ya doin'?" She tried a lighter note as Ida walked off to bestow a hug on Sam Ettinger.

"How do you think, Ella? All these beautiful young things have been clinging to my suit jacket. I feel like Rudolph Valentino."

"You keep this up, you'll look like Ray Milland in *The Lost Weekend.*"

"I think you're trying to tell me something, mother of mine. Don't worry about me. I'll be perfectly fine. I'll even applaud when you and Marcia do your vaudeville turns up there."

Should she announce the imminent arrival of Lois Katz? Better to go inch by inch.

"Sometimes, my son, for your information, you can be surprised. There are always younger people who show up. I know that's impossible for you to believe, but it is true." She sighed with the declaration.

"Ella, what present is in store for me now? In what pit were you digging up bones? What skeleton do I have to embrace this wonderful night?"

"Don't be silly. I just said it *can* happen. I didn't say it would." She looked out on the dance floor. Chip was bouncing along in the wake of Gertie Alperstein, survivor of the dance marathons, also known as Golden Gert—she did a mean wiggle and shake. And she was unstoppable. And there was

Marcia. Dancing again, or was it still, with Jack Ainsfeld? Talk about Valentino, Jack was the king of available males.

Long a widower, Jack had managed to avoid remarriage. But not before sampling almost all of the available Florida widows. And here was her Marcia taking him out of circulation for a whole evening. God knew Ella would hear about this tomorrow. Jack had money, he was handsome—cropped gray hair, light blue eyes—and he had managed to stay trim on a daily game of tennis. He was nuzzling Marcia, the lecher, nibbling at her bare shoulder, the gonif.

"Stay," she told Donald. As if he would leave the bar. "I'll be right back."

"I'm cutting in on you," sweetly sang she, tapping Jack on the shoulder.

"You want to dance with your own daughter?"

"No, dummy, I'm cutting in to dance with you. Marcia needs to rest a bit." Kissing Marcia and pushing her toward the side, away from the bar. She had sense enough to keep the siblings apart.

"You have a beautiful daughter, Ella. I could really go for her."

"Don't you think you're a little too old?" Ella asked hopefully.

"I'm in great shape and I'd be in better shape with a sweetie like your daughter. A pleasure."

"Jack, you just met her. Don't start having wet dreams on the dance floor. She needs a younger man."

"Ella, why don't you leave the decisions to Marcia, she's a grown woman. Besides, who says I'm asking her to marry me?"

Oh, oh. That was dangerous. Jack Ainsfeld never mentioned that word, not in a joke, not in a story, never. It was a forbidden word, banished from his vocabulary. Bad news.

"Jack, go ask Ida Alpert to dance. Wonderful dancer, she really is. And she looks like a dream tonight."

"Buttinsky, who asked you to be matchmaker? I'll dance

with who I want to dance with." Turned on the heel of his black Gucci loafers and strode off, leaving her in the middle of the dance floor.

"Chip Lowe to the rescue. But sit me down, Gertie has done me in."

She hugged him. "That lecher, Jack Ainsfeld, is after Marcia."

"Oh, come on, Ella, give him a break. He just wants a young chick for one New Year's Eve. What's so terrible about that?"

"I'll break his nose, he makes a pass at her."

"Why don't you let Marcia handle it herself, Ella? You keep forgetting she's over twenty-one." So does she, Ella thought.

She looked over at the doorway, past the balloons, in time to see Lois Katz walk in. Ella had left her name with the security cop on duty. "Oh, Lois is here already," she moaned to Chip. She hadn't prepared Donald at all.

"Darling, we're just getting ready to do the show, so you sit here with Chip and I'll introduce you to everyone when it's over." She squeezed Chip's hand and put it into Lois's. "See you later." Kiss, kiss.

Ran to fetch Marcia. From the clutches of Jack the Nibbler. Caught him at her shoulder again. "We'll see you after the show, Jack. Marcia has to get ready."

Walking backstage, she whispered to Marcia. "Do you really like Jack?"

"He's okay, Mom. He's not stupid and he's smooth."

"He's seventy if he's a day."

"Big deal."

Saw Donald moving away from the bar toward them. Avoid confrontations, she thought, and steered Marcia off to the left, skirting him. She'd take care of everything after the show. Everything.

Lenny Feldstein was waiting for her to get the acts straight and try out some of his shtiks. Terrible, but everyone was in such a good mood, who'd notice? She found her caftan on the chair where she left it and went into the bathroom to change out of the burgundy dress. Could already hear the first strains of Carmen Miranda, "Ay ay ay, I like you very much. . . . " Shirley Mittelman sounded fine. She moved closer to the stage so she could see Marcia play.

It was going well. Shirley got a lot of whistles, Marcia resounding applause, and Fanny Sussman was doing a great job on "The Syncopated Clock." Next, "Tonight We Love," or whatever it was called when Tchaikovsky first wrote it. Fanny was going to stay at the piano to accompany Ella, though they would use the full Lenny Feldstein orchestra for the Fiddler number.

Loved that moment before she went out to face the audience. I would have been a good trouper, she thought, if I'd started this years ago. Maybe a star, a real star, returning for the big number like Alice Faye in *Hello, Frisco, Hello.* A little flutter in the stomach but a lot of satisfaction when she walked out on the stage. First as Carol Channing singing "Hello, Dolly," followed quickly by "Some of These Days" a la Sophie Tucker. The older crowd really loved Sophie and she got a big round of applause. Ella loved to build and she worked her way into the Zip number from *Pal Joey.* Did her pretend strip using the caftan as if it were the fans of Sally Rand. Threw in "Shake Your Booties" in case there were any kids in the audience and to give them a little double entendre. Went offstage a moment, wiped the sweat from her face. Tied the pillow around her waist under the caftan, tucked her hair into the cap, and ran out for her big number, Tevye in *Fiddler on the Roof,* doing "If I Were a Rich Man." Doing it like Zero Mostel, like Topol in the movie, shaking her shoulders, her middle, lowering her voice an octave. They all stood to applaud this finale. She was a smash. Ready for the big time.

Back in the burgundy dress again. Face washed, makeup

fresh. Hugs from the women, the husbands, Chip with tears in his eyes.

"Ella, you are a joy. I'm a very smart man." She was too embarrassed to kiss him in front of the others. Put her hand on his cheek.

"Where's Marcia?" Looking for her.

"She's walking to the bar with Jack." Pointing.

All at the bar together. Oh, no. She had to tend to this. Fast. Gathering Chip and Lois she pulled them toward the bar. Could see Donald, could see him clearly. Surrounded by Bessie Goldstein, a cornucopia of bosom, two huge melons pressing into Donald's shoulder. Sarah Weinberg squeezing him from the right with her piercing voice, and Ida, the Barbie Doll, pushed to a side, little mussed peach, trying to maneuver back into position. The glass was still in his hand, tilting back, into his mouth. More poison. Getting numb, getting drunker, getting mean. She saw it happen before. Mean drunk, my nice son.

Marcia reached the bar before Ella could get there. She saw Donald rise, bow, say a few words. Saw Marcia pick up the glass and throw the vodka in his face. Saw an ice cube, one of them, slip down Bessie Goldstein's ample bosom. Saw Jack Ainsfeld raise his fists. Like Errol Flynn in *Gentleman Jim.*

Then she heard, "Thanks for the bath, bitch. Why don't you marry this old fool? Let him stick it to you once a month and live on an allowance for the rest of your life? Buy your clothes in Saks, have your hair done at Sassoon's, grow old in a year."

"And I'll send you cases of vodka, down on the Bowery where you'll be living when Ma has sense enough to throw you out."

"You cunt. You wouldn't know what sense means."

"You prick. I'm smarter than you ever gave me credit for."

Everyone was crowding the bar. Nothing like this had, not to her knowledge, ever happened at Bimini Towers.

She pulled them apart, got Jack Ainsfeld to lower his . . . dukes . . . looked at the sea of familiar faces.

"And that, friends, was the finale of the show which we prepared for you. Surprise. It's called Open Theater, and it's a big hit in New York. They do it in all the off-Broadway theaters. I hope you enjoyed it."

Bessie was in a bad state. Ella put an arm around her shoulder. "Darling, did you find the ice cube yet? Listen, Chip will take you out on the dance floor and you'll melt it out. Right, Chip?" Pleading with him as usual. Save the day.

"Ella, you're quite the moderator." Oh, she forgot Lois, touching her elbow. Jack was walking off with Marcia, patting her bare back, comfort in her moment of despair.

The villain was glaring at her. "It's all your fault, Ella. You set it up."

He was sobering a bit. She could see that too.

"You're some classic case, you know that?" Lois said to him. "You've got a major problem, buster."

"Who the hell is this, Ella, the squadron commander?"

"Oh, I forgot to introduce everyone. Lois Katz, my son, Donald Sager, from California. He's an artist."

"He sure is," Lois laughed. "I assume Ella means that Marcia is your sister, not your wife. Bet you do a pretty good job of wife beating too. Proud of yourself?"

"No." Ella hurried into the fray. "They really aren't like that. They're also not living together anymore."

"Thanks, Ella. I'm a free man. And I don't intend to be chained to any warden at the county jail."

"I think you're swell too," Lois responded.

"I'm glad the two of you are getting along so well." Ella felt she had to add these words. "I should leave you to get to know each other. Lois is divorced with two children. And a house. She's a feminist."

"You don't say?" Donald smirked at Lois.

Ella walked off holding her hands to her ears. She did not want to know what they were saying to each other. In old movies, Claudette Colbert and Clark Gable would start this way, and then they would fall in love. She hoped Lois and Donald could be just friends because she wanted him to go back to Holly eventually, if Holly would have him, of course. But the world was changing, they could have an affair. A brief encounter. She wished she didn't feel so guilty about Holly.

She looked up at the clock. How did she miss midnight? Those cheers she heard when Donald and Marcia were fighting were actually the celebration of the new year. Not a cheering throng for her children as she'd thought. *Oy.*

She went looking for Marcia. Again. There she was at a table with the Perlmutters and Jack Ainsfeld.

"Hi, can I sit down a minute?"

"Of course, darling, you deserve to sit. The show was wonderful." Sylvia beamed at her.

Abe's eyes were closed. Did he miss midnight too? she wondered. And was he awake for the show?

"I was just asking Marcia about that Open Theater," Sylvia smiled, "and she said it was another of your brainstorms, Ella. How did you ever manage it? It was so realistic."

"It's not easy to do, believe me. I got interested when I was in New York last summer. Staying with my brother the lawyer. He represents one of the producers. I showed Donald and Marcia how to do it. Like a preview, see? That group will be in Florida soon."

Marcia crossed her eyes, looked to the ceiling. Ella was off on a fantasy again. So what? Would she rather they all knew the truth? Only Ida Alpert next door could attest to the truth, but Ella could deal with Ida. Convince her what she'd heard before was the rehearsal. Ella smiled. Good idea, actually.

"Ella, I'm going to ask your permission to take Marcia to dance at the Fontainebleau. I've been invited to a party there by some important business associates." That added for Marcia's benefit, she supposed.

"In a minute I'll tell you, Jack. I just want to talk to Marcia alone first. A friend of hers, Lois Katz, came here tonight especially to see her. But I'll see what I can arrange."

She pulled Marcia off to the side. "You really want to go with him? You can tell me, I'll take care of it."

"Ma, maybe Donald is right. Maybe I should marry a man like Jack and let him take care of me."

"You dare to say that after the meetings we went to? What would Lois or Geraldine or Carole, what would they say to you? What would they say to me for allowing it? You don't think you could have a better life?"

"Frankly, Ma, I don't know. I wouldn't mind going to the Fontainebleau with him. You never know who I'll meet there. That's what you always used to tell me. Go. Go. Make an important contact. Just smile."

Ella *had* said that. A lot. These two, they brought up every word she had ever said before. Well, frankly, it wasn't a bad idea at that.

"Ma, I can take care of Jack. He's not going to rape me, for Chrissakes. I'm stronger than he is. So what's there to worry about? I have the key, I'll see you later. Okay?"

"I'll give my permission to Jack. But circulate there, don't stand by Jack's side. Maybe they'll think you're his daughter, you know? That's good." It was sounding better and the night might be saved.

They walked back to the table. Abe was still asleep. Jack was talking to Sylvia. "Here she is, Jack. Just take care of her and see she doesn't stay out too late. Goodbye, and goodbye Sylvia. I have to find Chip."

She'd spent little enough time with him tonight. Had they even danced? It was like the old days, with Phil. Worrying about the kids, so busy taking care of them, seeing too little of her husband. That was going to change. Hopefully these two would be off her hands, and soon. No repeat performance.

Chip wasn't on the dance floor. Oh, at the bar, there he was with Lois and Donnie. She walked over.

"Everything is fine with Marcia, Lois. She said hello and

sorry she couldn't stay, but we thought it would be better if she went somewhere else." She looked significantly at Donald.

"Before you ask, Ella, we're getting along fine. Chip is here to moderate or referee as the case may be," Donald informed her.

"I wasn't worried at all. Lois can take care of herself. Not like Marcia."

"Just keep the faith," Lois chirped. "We'll reform him. I've started already. He's not making my job so hard either."

Better Lois than Maureen O'Hara.

"I'm going to take Donald for a ride. My niece couldn't sit, so I asked Peggy Mahoney. You met her at my house, Ella. She's in the group. She's marrying a Cuban named Tino Gonzalez and they're cooking up a Cuban feast over there right now. Donald is deciding whether to come."

"You have to pull him by the hand, Lois. He doesn't make such quick decisions." She had maybe another hour at this party and she'd hardly talked to a soul yet. "Go, don't worry about me and Chip. We're okay. Here's the key, you can come in whenever you want." She kissed him goodbye.

She was on the dance floor with Chip when she realized what she'd done. "*Oy.* I gave them both keys. I can't get into the apartment till they get home."

Chip was laughing. "Ella, I almost never gamble; but I'll bet you did it deliberately."

Holding him. Did she? Did it matter?

Chip grinning still. "My place?"

Ready for the big time.

CHAPTER

26

NEW YEAR'S RESOLUTIONS. FIRST, TELL THEM ABOUT THE wedding date. Second, get Donald to call Sidney George at the university. Third, get Marcia to do . . . what? Fourth, call Leah, she'll be home from the cruise. Fifth, get Ida to talk more about the portrait, get Donald more work. Sixth, get an extra set of keys made.

She'd spent the whole night at Chip's apartment. And it was more passionate than ever before. Chip seemed to have unlimited energy and she found herself awakened in areas she thought were dead. She was a little embarrassed to be so excited at her age. Not a soul, not even Leah would know.

Came home at ten in the morning and woke Marcia, who assumed Ella had been asleep last night when she got in. Donald was not back yet.

"So, how was it last night? Meet anybody interesting?" She trilled the word.

"Actually, yes, Ma. A man in the music business. A friend of Jack's. He's down here on a Christmas vacation. Might have something for me in the classical division. Don't know exactly what he thinks I can do, but I have his phone number."

"How long will he be here?"

"Just another couple of days. I should think about it, though. Can't expect him to come up with anything if I don't know what to ask for."

"Right. Let's sit and think. What can you do?"

"If I knew so easily, Ma, I'd have told him last night. I

did take an advertising course at the New School. Maybe that division, with classical music. Public relations, promotion. . . ."

"Did you ask Jack about him?"

"He didn't know any more than I do. He wants to help me too. By marrying me."

"He proposed! I don't believe it. Jack never wanted to marry anybody. My God."

"Well, he wants to marry me, he said so."

"Marcia, you aren't seriously thinking about him as a husband, are you?"

"Oh, I'm thinking all right. In a very mercenary way. Just wondering if I'd be able to live with him, that's all."

"Come on, you can't do that. You're a young, beautiful woman. Look at yourself in the mirror. Already a man has offered you a big job in the music business, you can make yourself a career. . . ."

"Ma, what big career in the music business? He probably thinks I can be a secretary in some department or other and is wondering whether I take shorthand. You think because I'm your daughter he's going to make me president of the company?"

"Why not? You're a smart girl and you play the violin beautifully." Ella grinned at her. "Look, there must be something. Why don't we talk about it? Didn't Geraldine go back to work after lots of years, doesn't she have a career?" She said "career," not "job."

"It takes guts, Ma, and strength. I'm not sure I have either. Maybe Donald is right. I should just let Jack. . . ."

"Listen to me. Since when does your brother know everything? He hasn't lived with you for over twenty-five years, what can he know? Maybe he's a genius in the art field, but he doesn't do such a wonderful job in real life."

"I promise, Ma. I'll think. I don't have to make a decision today, I have his New York number. All I want to do now is soak in the tub. Hey, I was pretty good on the violin, right?"

An opening for her Jewish Mama number. "Darling, you weren't just good, you were wonderful. After you left, everybody there came up to me to say congratulations, and how beautiful you looked, where did you play your concerts? Yes, a lot of them thought you were professional."

Send her off to the bath contented. Add another New Year's resolution: Make them feel good about themselves. Very important. She thought she'd done that years ago. What happened? Who undermined her?

Walked inside to bathe in her own bathroom. Reminded herself to go downstairs and retrieve the caftan, hoped nobody had stolen it. Holly had selected it just for her. Made that trip to Morocco to choose fabrics. Stopped in New York, Ella had flown up to visit her there. A good chance to see Pam and Tommy and Marcia as well. Get everything in at once. Holly was beautiful. She got more so each year. Running her own company. Arranged for the financing, didn't ask Ella or even her own parents for any money. Ella hoped Donald was at least encouraging, even if he had no part in it. Supportive. After all, Holly was paying the bills. With dollars and cents. Buying the supplies he didn't use, buying the liquor he did.

She and Holly took a room together. Holly was such good company. A jolly person. So much like Ella herself. They went to the theater, they talked and talked and laughed at everything. Holly had dropped little hints about Donald and their relationship, but Ella had been slow to pick up the cues. Or, worse, hadn't wanted to. Wanted to think everything was lovely. Flew back to Miami feeling good, uplifted. Did Holly's own mother appreciate her as Ella did? Why not? The Rosens lived in Los Angeles and probably saw a lot of their daughter. Donald never mentioned them, didn't really like them. Too middle-class, he said. His own mother was a Queen of Romania, his father Prince of Bulgaria? Where did he get his ideas?

She climbed out of the tub and into her terry cloth robe and went padding into the kitchen to put the coffee on. Heard the key, heard the door open. The Prodigal Son returns.

Came out of the kitchen, smiling. "Did you have a good time?" Giving him a kiss.

"Yeah, it was okay. I liked the people. Not to mention the food. Probably spend the whole day farting from the beans."

"You slept over?" So innocent, the question.

"Now, now, not too many questions. There are a lot of rooms in that house. I could have slept in a guest room, right?"

"Look, Donald, do I care? Am I that kind of mother?"

"You're a funny kind of mother, Ella. How come you never mentioned that you and Chip were going to get married on the fifteenth of January?"

"What?" she cried. "Who?"

"It wasn't Chip who told me, Mom. Obviously, he told Lois, who passed it along in a throwaway sentence. When were you planning to tell me and Marcia?"

"What's the big deal? You've met Chip, you like him, you know we see each other. What more is there to say? Big fuss, a wedding. . . ."

"Ella, it's an important day for you. How many times have you been married? I know you. And I know it's not a decision you took lightly. You just didn't know you were going to be visited by your children. You're trying to figure out how to work around that, aren't you?"

"You're not always right, Donald. Chip wants to marry me with or without children. Nobody is left out. . . ."

"Who said anything about being left out? That's not the point. The point is, and let's be blunt, your two very grown children have returned to park themselves in your lap. And neither one of the two selfish brats is giving any thought to the way you feel at all, now are we?"

Marcia came out of the other bathroom. "What's going on?"

"Your mother and Chip are getting married on January fifteenth," Donald told her in the bluntest way he could.

Marcia stood vacantly. "Ma? So when were you going to

say something? What would you do, ask us to ride in the car with you to the rabbi's study and still pretend nothing was going to happen?"

"Do you mean I treat you like babies?"

"Well, it *is* unfair. . . ." Marcia was pouting.

"Oh, hey, fuck it"—that from Donald. But with a delicious grin. And taking her arm, squeezing it? "Ella? Listen. Mazeltov, eh? I hope it lasts a hundred years."

And then Marcia too, the tears suddenly bursting. "Oh, Ma! Oh, Ma!" Into Ella's arms, a squeeze.

Kvelling. Taking Donnie's hand too. Here, now, for the one moment at least, a family. Ella and her kids. Kvelling.

CHAPTER

27

"I'M BACK!" THE VOICE AT THE OTHER END OF THE PHONE sang to her.

"Leah! I'm so glad. You have no idea what's happened."

"Aren't you going to ask me about the cruise? It was so lovely. The very first day out. . . ."

"Leah, Marcia and Donald are here."

"What do you mean, Marcia and Donald? *Holly* and Donald, right?"

"I know who's here, Leah, you've been away. No alimony for Marcia so she sublet and came home to mama. Donald got kicked out by Holly. He, too, has no money and no place to go."

"Oh, wow. All this since I left?"

"You have no idea. Sit down. Are you sitting?"

"Ella, I sat down to make this call. What else?"

"Chip and I are getting married on the fifteenth of this month. January."

"Ella! I'm so happy. Irving!" she shouted the news into the other room.

"Tell Irving to wait. There's more. That's good, right? So now for the bad news. My two children are living here and my new husband is going to move in. With a stepdaughter whose clothes are littering the house, with a stepson who sleeps in the living room and spills vodka all over the floor."

"Calm down, Ella. We'll fix it. Don't we always fix everything?" She could imagine Leah's face, even over the phone. Sly grin, eyes crinkling.

"It's not so easy this time. But first of all, Chip wants Irving to be best man. And of course you'll be my matron of honor."

"And Ella, I'm going to have the pleasure of making the wedding supper at my place. I really am going to insist on that. You can be married here by Rabbi Waldman. Oh, I'm so excited. Are the kids there, can they hear what we're saying?"

"No, they're both out. In fact, another thing. Marcia is with Jack Ainsfeld. Imagine. He's taking her to dinner and to the movies. I think his little friend in the pants thinks he's in love." Ella laughed. Leah giggled. Things didn't seem quite so bleak now after all.

"I think I found a job for Donald, teaching art. But he can't know it's my suggestion. You'll have to help me with that too. We'll plan what to say."

"Maybe I'll drive over first thing in the morning. We'll talk in the car."

"Good. So, what about the cruise?"

"You don't need to hear about my good time. It was nice. Even some single men, if you hadn't found Chip I could have brought you a live one. Ida will shoot herself when I tell her. I warned her she'd be sorry if she didn't book this cruise. I'll rub it in, she'll cry till next New Year's."

"You must be exhausted. Tell me, was it as much fun as our trip to Europe?"

"Can you achieve Paradise twice in a lifetime? How could it, such a question."

"I can't wait to see how you look. Come early, don't forget."

"I promised. I'll be there. I'll take a pill, get a good night's sleep. Oh, Ella, if I can sleep at all! I'm so happy for you!"

Kvelling still. Ella Sagersdorf, up to her tushie in tsooris. So how come she's so bursting with joy?

CHAPTER

28

"DONALD, IT'S THE PHONE FOR YOU."

Shirley Mittelman, a convert to portraits. Ella knew that once Sylvia Perlmutter was committed, the army would follow. Shirley today, Rose Wolfinger tomorrow, who knew how far it would go? Out of Bimini Towers and into the Sisterhood. She'd call Rabbi Waldman's wife, let it drop. An item for the newsletter, dear, something like that.

But this could run out, or Donald could get bored, so she'd better get that teaching job for him. Where was Leah? She expected her to come early.

Donald finished the call, was looking over at her. "Ella, did you arrange this? Another of your biddies. I feel like the new hairdresser."

"I know you'll find it hard to believe but I had nothing to do with it."

"It is hard to credit."

"Donald, if you had the perfect life, what would it be? Did you ever think about that?"

"Sure. I'd have a rich patron who would give me money, like in the Renaissance. I'd just sit there and paint whatever I wanted to paint."

"But you can do that now. Holly makes enough money."

"I think I forgot how to paint. No, don't look at me like that. It's a state of mind, and I got rusty. I have to find myself before I try to go back. Holly won't have a halfway attempt."

"You'll find yourself. You're a special person. And you

know, you used to be a great teacher, you really could get people thinking and interested. Wouldn't that be a good thing to do? Maybe teach in a college for a bit?"

"I'm too old to start teaching now. Who in hell would have me?"

"Donald, maybe we could check it out. I'll ask around. I'm very friendly with some young professors."

"*You're* friendly with professors? Ella, you're putting me on. What do you discuss?"

"Art in the Marketplace." The title of an article in last month's *Miami Herald.* And then out the door and downstairs before he could question her further.

Leah came bounding through the glass doors as she reached the lobby. They held on and hugged.

"Let's ride around. I'm happy to be back in my car again. And I have to go to the supermarket. There's nothing in the apartment and Irving is starved."

While they stood at the door, the elevator expelled its lone passenger.

"Marvin, you're going to business so late? You look wonderful. Do you know my friend Leah? Leah, this is Marvin Silverman from the floor below me. He works at Burdine's. He's an executive."

He smiled and shook Leah's hand.

"Did you have a nice New Year's?" Didn't notice him at the Bimini Towers party.

"Great."

"Marvin, I've got some visitors, hope they aren't disturbing you. I mean the extra noise. Imagine, my children surprised me. Heard I was getting married in a couple of weeks and came here. My son's from California and my daughter's from New York City."

Ella saw Leah's eyebrows rise in anticipation.

"In fact, Marvin, would you be free to have dinner with us tomorrow night? I don't know many young people here. My

Donald is an artist and my Marcia a musician." Make them both professionals.

"That would be lovely, Mrs. Sagersdorf. What time do you want me to come?"

"Is seven okay with you? With the job, I mean."

"It's perfect. I'll be there. May I bring wine? White or red?"

"Whatever you like to drink, dear."

He rushed out.

"Why did you do that, Ella? Is he going to solve your problems?"

"Leah, he's an executive. Who knows what kind of jobs he could get for Marcia at the store? And he's a lot younger than Jack Ainsfeld."

"He dresses with style," Leah admitted. "But I still am puzzled, dear."

"Well, you'll find out everything because you'll be there. We'll send Chip and Irving to the trotters. I'll try to think of someone for Donald."

"I'd gladly be his date," Leah offered.

"Don't be ridiculous. I'll call this woman I met recently. She doesn't have children so we don't have to worry about a sitter." Carole Cavalcanti. Bright and pretty, and liked to talk. The evening would be lively. Get Carole's phone number from Geraldine.

"I'm just thinking, Ella. I heard of a private school, for the children of rich Cubans. Maybe Donnie could teach there. They probably pay well. You want me to find out more?"

"Sure. The more we find out, the better it will be."

Leah was true to her word, though Ella hoped this Señora Lopez spoke English. She didn't know whether she could carry it off in pidgin Spanish.

"Listen, Ella," Leah suggested. "I'll make the appointment, pretend I'm your social secretary. I'll say you are a professor from somewhere. You can take it from there when you talk to her."

"Let me call Carole Cavalcanti first. Imagine, she's a marine biologist. I didn't know they had women in the marines."

Carole picked up on the first ring, and did indeed remember Ella. "Tomorrow night at seven? I'd love to see you and Marcia again. It's not a party, is it? I hate big parties. What's the address again? . . ."

Ella wore the Sybil Churchill wardrobe. Leah was amazed. "Perfect. You're a different person. I hardly know you."

"My dear friend, transport me without further discussion to the domicile of Señora Lopez. I shall work my magic on her. Drive on, Macduff." She giggled.

Leah stopped the car in front of a very elegant house. "Boy, these Cubans must have a lot of money. Do you think this is the school or Mrs. Lopez's home?"

Ella didn't know and was a bit awed by the imposing splendor of the house. This was no Sidney George situation, she could tell. "I'm a little scared, Leah. It doesn't seem as easy as the other day."

Ella walked up the white steps and rang the bell. Chimes, naturally. She expected a butler in livery to open the front door. She was hardly prepared for the young, dark-haired boy.

"Hi, my mother was expecting you. Are you Mrs. Churchill? Related to Winston?"

"Cousin," she said without blinking. "May I come in?"

"Sure, the study. That door." He pointed vaguely and ran off.

Ella walked toward a closed door. She sucked in her breath and knocked.

"Venga," a voice seemed to say.

Ella entered a small sitting room. A very dark room with a thick drape pulled shut and a small lamp providing the only light. Seated on the white couch was an enormous woman, quite gray, looking amazingly like Sidney Greenstreet. That boy was obviously a change-of-life baby. And this was not the house of a poor refugee.

"Señora Lopez. I am the professor from Vassar, Sybil

Churchill. Come to talk to you about placing a very talented young man in your school. On the faculty, of course."

"Of course." She had a lovely lisp and her eyes glittered. "He is qualified for my group?"

"Yes. From what I understand. It is art, right?"

"Of course." Glittering smile once again. "Does he have experience?"

"Oh, yes."

"He is a refugee from Cuba?"

"No, but he has a fine intelligence."

"Ah, intelligence. Yes. He uses the British or German system?"

"Actually, Italian is his period."

"Italians were not very good in intelligence."

Ella was surprised. "Oh, I know some very smart Italians. And throughout history. . . ."

"We will change history. I like the British system myself. I think James Bond was wonderful. Is your young man like James Bond?"

She didn't know a painter named Bond. And this woman was very disconcerting. She seemed so intense and at the same time so remote.

"I don't know this Bond. Donald Sager is his own man, you know, his own style."

"That is what I like. Individual style. Is he very stealthy?" The woman adjusted the folds of her chiffon dress. It was rose-colored and rather elegant for the afternoon. Probably a Cuban custom to dress this way, Ella thought. "Does he have a code?"

"He's very ethical, of course." If that is what she meant? Strange questions this woman asks. And not a word on whether he'd be a good teacher.

"Ethics are on our side. But we must be very careful. The other side is trying to infiltrate the organization. We must select our people very carefully."

"Oh, is there another school? Well, I didn't know that. I'm just seeing you." Leah hadn't prepared her for the bizarre Señora Lopez.

"School is out. The real world infiltrates. Armed with the finest minds, the keenest intelligence, we will prevail."

"Yes, of course. But do you want to see his credentials?" Ella wished she could pin down this woman, get some idea of how much time was left, how soon they would fill the job.

"Don't rush me. This is a dangerous job. It takes a careful decision. Very careful." The woman frowned and hissed the words at Ella.

At that moment, the door opened. A young and very beautiful woman entered.

"Ah, you must be Mrs. Churchill. I am Señora Lopez. I've been waiting for you in the study. I see you have met my mother-in-law."

She turned to the older woman. "Mamacita, andiamos. Mrs. Churchill and I must talk privately." She waved goodbye to the older woman, who lifted her chiffon off the sofa and exited. Stealthily.

"Now," she turned to Ella, "you've come about the possible faculty position."

When Ella finally got down to the interview, it went well. But it was clear that Donald was going to have to appear in person for such things.

"Sure, that's logical," Leah said, giving it serious thought. "But how do we even get Donald to *call* these people. And where *are* his credentials and slides?"

"I can't ask him. I know he'll explode. Leah, what if I call Holly? She's so reasonable. She can give me the story on the telephone. I'll find out if there are slides. I'm sure he didn't bring them along. He has such a small suitcase. She can airmail them."

"Better we should airmail Donald back to Holly. How is he going to live without her, Ella? It's a disaster."

"I know. You think I don't wish they'd get back together? You of all people know how I feel. But can I just mark him 'Return to Sender' and put him in a box? He has to do something first, right?"

"You better call Holly from my place. We don't want Donald to eavesdrop on this conversation."

"And we have to plan what I'm going to make for dinner tomorrow. Not too Jewish. You know, chic, continental. Let's think about it."

"Sweetheart, I'll make you a quiche to start. With the drinks. That's elegant. You can take it from there." Leah baked. Ella had never tried to. Hated the oven, a phobia. Top of the stove or broil. Bought cakes and breads in the stores. So what?

"What about veal goulash with saffron rice? That's not too Jewish. And a salad with Italian dressing. I'll throw in a piece of Roquefort."

"Do you want me to bring a bottle of Crown Royal also?" Leah asked.

"Darling, I hate to mention it. But nobody except people our age drinks that. Donald takes vodka, Marcia Scotch. Who drinks rye nowadays? I'll get some gin, some sherry, wine in case Marvin forgets. Leah, why are we worrying about booze? Better we should plan how to get Donald to the telephone."

"Okay," Leah said. "First you call Holly. If there are no credentials, there's no job, there's no next phone call necessary."

"Leah," she pleaded, "there have to be credentials. What was he doing these past twenty years?"

CHAPTER

29

HOLLY WAS IN HER OFFICE. SHE SPELLED OUT THE PLACES, the galleries, the awards. It was actually a pretty impressive list. She'd find the slides, make copies, and mail them off special delivery air mail. Would take a couple of days. She sounded gentle, pleased. Or so it seemed to Ella.

A weight lifted. He had credentials.

"Ella, I'll type up the list, I'll make xeroxes, don't worry," Leah said. "Now we have to figure out a way to get him to make the phone call. Wait, I know. The dinner. Okay, he can get mad at you and Marcia, but not at me, and not in front of Marvin Silverman and Carole. No, he won't do that. At least it will sink in."

"But don't make him feel guilty, Leah."

"I like Donnie and he likes me. I'll be a diplomat; it will be my idea, something I did. Ella, he'll never know you were the momzer behind it."

Leah drove her home with the packages. She walked in to find Marcia crying in the middle of the kitchen. Over a cup of herbal tea.

She dropped the packages. "Darling, what's the matter?"

"Remember that man in the music business who might have a job for me? He called here. Jack gave him the number. He has a job all right. In his bedroom!"

Ella's mouth opened. The skunk, her sweet daughter, what right did he have? "Marcia, what exactly did he say? Are you sure you didn't misunderstand him?"

"I didn't have my earplugs in, Ma. I know what he said.

He's very attracted to me. He wants to set me up in an apartment, right here in Miami Beach, and come down on weekends. I guess I can file my nails the rest of the time."

"He actually said . . . I mean, talked about sex? Maybe he just wanted you to, like, apartment sit for him."

"Mother, you are impossible. He wants to get laid. L-a-i-d. Go to bed with me. Without his wife around. Does that sound innocent to you?"

No, it didn't sound innocent. Not at all. But he's the adulterer, the culprit, the criminal. Maybe we should teach him a lesson. How?

"Marcia, what if we screw him? Let him take the apartment, then we call in a locksmith and he won't be able to get in the door. We'll show him."

"Ma, if he can't get in, he'll stop paying rent. Didn't that occur to you?"

"Make him pay a year's rent in advance." Nobody could accuse Ella of being slow on her feet.

"He'll call the police, he'll sue me, something, Ma."

"You really think so? In front of his wife and his friends, he'll make a fuss? Better to lose a couple of thousand bucks, who would know?"

"You really are desperate, Ma, aren't you?"

"Darling, I want you to find a place when you're good and ready. I'm happy to have you here now. Don't forget that."

She threw her arms around Ella's neck. "I love you, Ma."

"And me you, darling. Listen, before I forget. I'm making a dinner party tomorrow night. At seven. Don't make other plans. I'm inviting Carole Cavalcanti and also my neighbor, Marvin Silverman, from downstairs. And Leah. And Donald." She said that last name very, very quietly, hoping Marcia would miss it. "Chip and Irving have a date together."

"Okay. I'm going out on the terrace now."

Boy, that apartment sounded good to Ella. Fool the old putz. Let him get the apartment for Marcia and when he comes to collect his weekend, let him find Ella in the bed.

Nice, plump, zoftig cookie waiting for the music man. Boy, would he sputter. He'd put his hand over his heart. Press, groan. Quick, quick, he'd tell her, my pills. First you sign this contract turning the apartment over to my daughter, rent paid for the next twenty years. She just happened to have the paper ready. Ha!

At least in her fantasies, Ella thought, there was always hope. Springing eternal. Certainly in her breast.

Guadalupe, the maid, was coming tomorrow. She'd ask Marcia to straighten up a little beforehand. She wouldn't want Lupe to know how messy the house had been in her absence.

Maybe she'd get her to make an apple pie. Lupe made wonderful apple pies. She'd learned that and how to make delicious chopped liver, Jewish style, from her last employer.

Chip would have to buy the apples. No car, couldn't just run out now. Even if she had a car, didn't drive. Never important in New York City. Here it's a calamity. Her brothers all drove. Hmmm. Why not the daughter? She'd asked her mother once. Because I thought you would have a chauffeur, my beauty, her mother had answered.

Told Marcia the same thing. Dumb promises. At least Marcia *had* learned to drive.

Phone rang. Lois Katz wanting to invite Marcia to the next meeting. Ella began to feel guilty about asking Carole instead of Lois for dinner. Hoped Carole wouldn't mention the evening to Lois.

Guilty about Lois. Guilty about Holly. Guilty about Marcia. Guilty about Donald. Try Chip, try her mother, her father, try Phil. Yes, maybe Phil.

Pile it on. Life's grandest comfort, a load of Jewish guilt.

CHAPTER

30

THE APARTMENT WAS SPOTLESS. LUPE HAD SURPASSED HER most outstanding earlier performance. Everything glowed. She had even buffed Donald's desert boots with a suede brush.

"I don't theenk he ever do this, missus." She was probably right.

Leah came early, put the quiche in the oven to warm.

Only the *kinder* were not there. "Leah, I'll plotz if they forget."

"Why should they forget? They don't know what you have in store."

The door opened. In they came, together for once. Accidentally, of course.

Cries, squeals, Leah was being embraced, observed, interrogated. Ella was delighted to fade into the background and just look at them. Marcia was fine, very casual, jeans again. She hoped Marvin Silverman appreciated that look. Donald in his chinos. He seemed to own nothing else. Those and white sox. Only white sox. Never a color. Why? He didn't have athlete's foot as a child.

"You'll protect me from my mommy, won't you Leah?" Donald was twinkling at her. Little did he know. She hoped Leah had a plan of attack.

Donald moved into the kitchen to get a glass. "They're all in here, on the bar, dear. With the ice cubes in the bucket."

She'd done her company number. Got out every piece of silver. Buckets, platters, cigarette holders, candy dishes, wineglasses (from Spain), ice tongs, the works. On the side table, set up as a bar, everything was displayed.

"Hey," Donald said, "it seems so formal. Am I dressed okay? Who's coming, for Chrissakes?"

The clock struck seven as the buzzer sounded. Ella guessed it was Marvin Silverman. He looked like a person who was always on time. She opened the door.

He leaned down to peck at her cheek. "Hi, Mrs. Sagersdorf, I brought some white wine. You can chill it in the refrigerator before dinner." Of course, he wouldn't forget.

"Leah," she ordered, turning into the kitchen, "make the introductions."

"Marvin, this is Donald. Donald, Marvin." They shook hands.

Ella returned to take over. "And Marvin dear, this is my daughter, Marcia." Smiles all around.

"Carole will be here any minute. Let me get you a drink, Marvin. What will you have?"

"Martini, thanks." Dammit, a martini, naturally she didn't know how to make one.

"I'll fix it for you." Donald to the rescue. Leave it to him to know how to fix all kinds of drinks.

They sat there chatting amiably, all very subdued and formal, when the bell rang again.

"That's Carole, I'm sure," Ella called out.

In she came wearing the same chinos as Donald, the same white sox, the same desert boots. Looking very tanned, very scrubbed, very pretty.

"Hi, don't anyone get up. I had a fantastic day, was out on a boat all afternoon. It's part of a course I teach. What a way to make a living!"

Well, isn't she cheerful. Good idea to have invited her. Did Donald look a little interested?

"Carole Cavalcanti, you don't know my friend Leah, or my son, Donald. And this is my neighbor, Marvin Silverman. He's an executive at Burdine's."

"Nice for you, Marvin," Carole observed, "but doesn't it get you down, being inside all day in this climate?"

"I like it, Carole. My skin doesn't take to the sun and I actually enjoy what I'm doing. Sometimes I swim in the early mornings. I think I saw you in the pool one morning, Don." He turned to him. Donald nodded.

"Could be. My mother throws me out very early in the day. You might have seen me sketching. Trying to make her friends look like real people. No offense, Leah. You know I don't mean you."

"What do you do, Carole?" Marcia remembering to be a hostess.

"I'm a marine biologist. And you?"

"Just trying to find myself," she replied. "I'm interested in music, going to try to get something in that field."

"Do you have a big music department at the store, Marvin?" Ella was always ready to rush in.

"Yes, but I don't think you'd want to work as a salesclerk, do you, Marcia?"

"Oh, no," she said quickly. "I had something a bit more esoteric in mind. I'd like to work for a music company or something like that. I may even go back to school."

"That's a good idea," Carole said. "School is wonderful. I love the atmosphere."

Well, Ella thought. An unexpected bonus. Good setup for Leah's pitch later. She looked over at her friend. They winked at each other. Evening was going well.

Leah went into the kitchen and came back with the quiche. Ella had forgotten, of course. She always got interested in what people were saying and forgot to check on the food.

"I never liked the academic atmosphere much," Donald said.

"Maybe it was the wrong place. Or the wrong subject. What's your field?" Carole asked.

"I'm a painter. I teach art every once in a while."

"I love art," Marvin piped in. "And music, too." He turned

to Marcia. "In fact I have an enormous record collection. Every opera in the world. I have at least one recording of each. There are some conductors I don't like, however. I just will not have Furtwängler in my home."

He pronounced it Fortvongler. Ella didn't have a clue who that was, though she was sure it was a German. Probably a Nazi. She hoped Marvin didn't drive a Volkswagen either, or type on an Olympia. How far did he go? She liked Günter Grass and he was German. Loved his book, *The Tin Drum*. Maybe Marvin had a list of good Germans and bad Germans. Perhaps Grass would be on the good list.

"I go to the opera whenever I can, also. Whenever I'm due in New York City, I schedule the trip during the season. And I go to Texas and San Francisco. Victoria de los Angeles makes me cry."

Ella stared at him. What a strange, passionate boy Marvin was. You never really got to know your neighbors. Especially one as young as Marvin in a house with tenants as old as those in Bimini Towers.

"Marvin dear, you gave such an impassioned speech. And you are so right about de los Angeles," Leah responded to him. Leah knew. She was a good pianist and had taught music in New York City, at Music and Art, for years. You had to be good to teach there.

"I like the opera too, Marv. Wish there was a company in Miami," Marcia added.

"I know. It's a crime that we have so little culture here. So little *real* culture."

Ella went into the kitchen. Got everything ready, ticked it off, started to put the dishes on the table. Well, they had already eliminated a job for Marcia. Marvin was too negative, it wouldn't work, selling in the music department. Maybe Marcia would like him as a person, as a date. He was a little stiff, but nice looking. Okay looking. Neat dresser. Carole, on the other hand, now who wears chinos to go out to dinner? Wait, Ella, she thought, this is what she had to learn. It doesn't matter if you don't wear a dress. Right? *Oy*. It takes so long to get through my brainwashed head.

Leah had followed her. "What can I do? Are you putting everything on the table? They seem to be getting along quite well. Nobody is fighting, so far everyone is agreeing. That's because we haven't discussed politics or sex." Leah grinned.

"When are you going to mention the phone calls?"

"Ella, I have to find the right moment. I can't just say, everyone shut up, I have an announcement, now can I?"

Why not? Ella wondered. Why can't you always say exactly what you wanted to say? Pussyfoot, inch around the point, don't hurt anyone's feelings. Silly.

She brought the casserole to the table, followed it with the rice bowl. She had made an interesting salad of string beans, pine nuts, avocados, and endive. She knew Marcia would be impressed.

"Okay, everyone, come and get it," Ella beckoned the brood. Seated them carefully so that Marcia sat next to Carole and faced Marvin. Donald sat next to Marvin and faced Carole. Ella and Leah at opposite ends of the table.

Carole and Marcia were talking about the speech on sexuality. The one Andrea Dworkin gave. Donald asked for further amplification, that's the word he used.

"Pass me the plates, I'll serve all of you," Ella called out.

"Pretty unconventional views on sexuality," Donald said.

"The world is changing a lot, Donald," Carole told him.

"Would you like more rice, Marvin?" Ella asked.

"Yes."

"My choices have been pretty straight. I like heterosexual behavior." Her Donald was right.

"Have you tried any other kind?" Carole asked him.

"Actually, not," Donald said.

"What about you, Marcia? Gee, I hope I'm not embarrassing you in front of your mother and Leah." Carole was a nice, sensitive girl.

"No, but I'm sorry to say I've only tried it with men."

"Leah and I were saying how we would have lived differently today."

"Oh," Carole said, "that's interesting. So you and Leah have a special relationship. Wow, you're very liberated women. Very much so." Carole beamed at Ella. "It's unusual to find women of your age who admit to it."

"Admit to what?" Ella asked.

"Well, to lesbian feelings."

Ella blushed. Her cheeks matched Leah's. "What lesbian feelings?"

Leah added, "We never wanted to be anything more than just friends."

"Oh," Carole said, "but are you sure? If you were brought up in a different time when it was acceptable, perhaps your love which is emotional would also turn physical. Don't you see it's possible?"

"My mother?" Donald laughed. "You've got to be kidding. Ella and Leah? Too much."

"We don't even look like lesbians," Leah said.

"What do lesbians look like?" Carole asked.

Leah was quick to respond. "Well, they are very big and heavy and look like men."

"Do I look like a man?" Carole asked.

"Of course you don't," Leah answered. "Just because you aren't wearing a dress. . . ."

"But I am a lesbian." She said it firmly. The words floated across the table, tapped each person on the shoulder, and rested.

"You are?" It was Marcia who finally voiced the question.

"Yes, I am. And it took me a long time to admit it, but I like the way it feels to have people know. It's a sharing of part of myself."

"I always thought it was because you didn't find the right man, that your sex life wasn't right. If you had the real thing, hey, Marvin?" Donald turned to ask the question.

Marvin blushed. He dropped his eyes. "Since we're being

honest, I wouldn't know. I'm gay myself and I've had plenty of men."

A memorable dinner party, Ella. The inauguration of gay liberation in Miami. Here at Ella Sagersdorf's dinner table. Always in the avant garde. This is the way her life was going. She's making matches for her children. She should change the seating arrangement. Put Marvin with Donald and let Marcia go home with Carole. Get them out of the apartment, at least.

"Well, this is very interesting to me, really. I don't think— Leah, am I right?—that anyone has ever been so honest with us. Usually they don't say anything to older people because we're supposed to be so shocked, right? But what could shock now? I'm just glad you found a happy way to live. Are you both happy?" Ella smiled at them.

"Not one hundred percent, Mrs. Sagersdorf, actually," Marvin admitted.

Sure, Marvin, she thought. You look at Marcia and you wonder if you've made a serious mistake, hanging out just with men.

"I wish I had a mother I could talk to," Marvin went on. "One who would listen to the truth. She doesn't know and that kills me, really."

Ella wouldn't breathe a word. Mrs. Silverman was probably sitting around some table now, taking down phone numbers of sweet young things, preparing to send them on to her darling Marvin who was still "holding out" (she had used that word herself and now she shuddered recalling the legions of those "holdouts").

"Do you have a steady, Marvin?" she asked gently.

"Actually, I do, Mrs. Sagersdorf. We share the condominium. Victor has the other bedroom. We believe in separate rooms. It's healthier."

Separate rooms. Ella believed in separate *apartments* and couldn't get her wish. "I never saw Victor, did I?"

"You probably did and just didn't realize we lived together. Why would you? They don't know at the store either."

"My friends at school know," Carole said. "I really don't keep it a secret, though I also don't wear a button saying *I am a Lesbian*." She laughed.

"Maybe we should all wear buttons," Marcia said. "It would be helpful."

It certainly would, Ella felt. Maybe even a little colored ribbon.

"And I'm really a very nice person, Ella. And I haven't tried to seduce your daughter."

Oy vay. She said it, Ella told herself. I never said, never thought.

"You must think I'm an antique. I know a lot of things, Carole. Of course, you don't seduce my daughter. I'll bet you're not that kind of person. You don't go around seducing anybody."

Carole's eyes twinkled. "Don't be so sure. I've got a pretty good crush on you."

Leah tittered. Ella could swat her.

"Sure, I'm everybody's darling," Ella said. "Who can resist a big fat Jewish mama?"

They all laughed. Even Donald, she noticed. Maybe she could get the talk away from everybody's sex life and onto something safe like movies, or have you read any good books . . . ?

"Something you said before interested me, Carole. About teaching and how you enjoyed it. Didn't that interest you, Leah?" Was that pointed enough? Leah looked at her glassy-eyed. Get on with it, she glared at her.

"Yes, I was thinking about that," Leah managed. "Especially what you said about teaching. A friend of mine mentioned that there are, well, possibilities for some jobs. Here in Florida, for artists. Or for teachers of art." She stopped, frowning. It hadn't come out right. Not casual enough and certainly not specific. No mention of a phone call.

"Donnie, they'd be perfect for you. Do you think you'd get in touch with these people if I asked you?"

God, Ella thought, that was blunt.

"I don't know, Leah, let's talk about it some other time. This discussion with Carole and Marvin interests me more."

Oh, great. She arranged this evening. She picked the people. So that they could support Leah in the phone call maneuver. Now it was out of her hands.

"But what Leah says. . . ." Ella tried.

"No, Ma, Donald is right. You know about my experience with Charlie." Marcia turned to the others. "My last boyfriend came out, and he was too cruel to explain anything to me, so I would like to discuss this with both of you. . . ."

"People are cruel," Carole offered. "It has nothing to do with gay or straight. Your last boyfriend was just a shithole."

Oh, boy, Donald had a friend. Now she had probably unleashed the torrent of his dirty words.

"Does anybody want more meat, or some salad?" No use, Ella knew. They'd go on, explaining about gay and straight, at her dinner table. Maybe Chip and Irving should have been here. She'd love to see Irving's face.

"But, Donald, maybe for a second, you. . . ." Leah was trying again, bless her.

"Leah, I love you, but shut up for now. We'll talk about it some other time. And pay attention, you might learn something in your old age. Who knows, you might divorce Irving, Ella will cancel her marriage to Chip and you can be our daddy."

Very funny. When she thought of living with Leah, like in her Italian dream, it had nothing to do with sex. Just a companion. Anyway, what did two women do together? She knew if she asked that, Carole would answer. She heard how two men did it. People talked about it openly and it seemed obvious. But what did women do? What could you put where?

What was she hearing? Carole was being specific. Nice, but specific. Careful, but specific. Talking about how it felt. *Oy gevalt.* Leah had to listen to this too. Two nice Jewish ladies. Sixty-five years of age. Learning. Next she'd have Marvin tell his side. Round out the whole dinner. Everybody know what everybody else did. Next time she'd ask a eunuch. Be impartial altogether.

Leah was leaning forward. She was fascinated. What canasta hand could beat this combination? Tomorrow, Ella would think of another way to get Donald to the phone. For tonight, well, for tonight she'd chalk it up as another radical experience.

CHAPTER

31

QUIET IN THE APARTMENT. AND SO THEY SAT, THE THREE OF them alone. Sometimes it seemed to Ella that her children did not want to leave her side. That they would be content from this day forward to climb onto her lap, take a little sip from the nipple, and make their way back to the womb. A charming picture. She realized it did not bode well.

Maybe they were catatonic. Ella had seen an interesting documentary film once which showed various types of mentally ill children. Did they look like hers?

It was probably her fault. She had great expectations and what happened? Leah suggested she have a heart-to-heart with both of them. Give them direction. If she gave any stronger directions, they'd hang a traffic light around her neck.

"Donald, a very odd thing happened," Ella began.

He looked up from his book. "On the way to the Forum?"

"No. It actually happened to Leah. What she started to tell you herself. She has some very intellectual friends and they were talking about the situation in the colleges down here. One of them teaches at the university and his name is Sidney George. He was saying that he has an opening for an art teacher, and another friend of Leah's, a woman named Sybil Churchill, she recommended you."

"What recommend? For what?"

"For the Art Department job, of course. See, Leah has talked about you a lot."

"All the time she was on the cruise, or before that when I lived in California?"

Better to ignore that. To answer would be madness.

"Donald, the thing is, I'm afraid this Churchill woman really gave you a big buildup. And Mr. George is quite anxious to talk to you."

"About what?"

"I just said what. About a job in the Art Department."

"They'd be hiring for next fall, Ella. What do I need that for?"

A good question. Find a because.

"Because it could make you feel better. You could be proud of yourself, stand on your own feet, don't count on Holly. Maybe it will give you a place to work, a studio, you'll start to paint again. I mean really paint, not putting down the faces of my friends."

"I'm earning money from your friends, as it happens. In fact I opened a bank account yesterday. Hell, I'll have a new career: Donald Sager, Painter of Israelites. Don't you think that has possibilities?"

Marcia didn't even look up from her magazine. Her body was in the room, her mind elsewhere. Obviously. Such a good opening for a crack at her brother and she ignores it. Something is happening, Ella thought.

"Marcia, you have nothing to say?"

"Ma, what's to say? I'm just wondering what you've planned for me?"

That's it. That's the final nail in the coffin. "I have nothing planned for you, Marcia, and I wish I did. I'm so tired of trying to plan my own day, week, maybe month, that I don't have time to change your diapers anymore."

Ah, now she had their attention. "I did this for you before. I want you both to do things by yourselves now. Don't either one of you have an idea, a simple idea of what you're going to do? If I died tonight, would you move in with Leah, let *her* fix things, make it nice? Would you sit by her side, eat at her table? Would you notice I was gone or just that you were in a different apartment? If I lived in a home, if I were a sick woman, if I had no money, then what would you do?"

They looked startled. She hadn't meant to yell at them, but she wished they'd show some initiative, move around, do *something* to indicate they were alive.

"I can't figure out why we're this way, Ma," Marcia said. "You're independent, you do your thing, you're tough. I *don't* understand it, I really don't."

"I understand," Donald decided. "She wants us to be motivated. To be involved in a job, and to earn money. Most of all I think she wants us to have separate apartments."

"Why do you turn it around so I come out the bad one?" Ella said. "Like I'm kicking you out? That's not what I mean. Not at all."

Yet she *didn't* say what she meant, not to the children. How come it was easier for her to talk to Pam and Tommy than to her own two? If she said what she really felt, maybe they wouldn't love her anymore. The rational part said, so what? Other people love you, does the whole world have to love Ella Sagersdorf? Then the other part, the part closest to the heart, says if my own children don't love me, what have I got? She knew a lot of cases, a surprising amount in fact, where the children actually hated their parents. She could not understand how the animosity started. These other parents seemed equally proud, equally fierce in their love. How come her own didn't seem to hate their mother?

Donald stood up. "Okay, Ella. I'll talk to the guy. What's his name? You probably went to great lengths to arrange this, and I don't want to let you down again."

"What lengths? I didn't do a thing. It's Leah's friend, don't forget to mention her name. Sybil Churchill."

Ella never discussed the wedding plans. Not since the one time that Donald had brought it up, not since then had words been said. She had to plan. She had to do it in front of them. Flowers, the rabbi, the honeymoon, everything, it couldn't happen by magic. If Ella didn't do it, it wouldn't get done.

"It's almost the fifteenth of January," she said aloud.

"What's that?" Marcia asked.

"Well, it's the day Chip and I. . . ."

"Oh, Ma, I'm sorry, I forgot. Listen, let's change places. You be the daughter. I'll be the mother and I'll take care of your wedding. Just tell me when, where, how many people, and," she smiled, "how much you want to spend."

"Leah is making the wedding. Call her."

"Hey, Ma, you know what? I'm going to throw a shower for you. What a great idea. We'll have it here. We'll ask relatives. Whoever lives down here. Do you have a list?"

Let's see, she thought. Do I include Phil's people? We were very friendly. Why not? And her own family? There was old Aunt Gussie, who lived with her daughter Sophie. Cousin Mary and her sister Hannah. There was Charlotte and Jack, but they were a couple. Did Marcia want to invite only women? Larry and Ruth. Muriel and Norman. Just the wives. Cousin Esther, Sadie Melman, Julia from Philadelphia, Ruby from upstate. Flossie, Helen, and Gussie Birnbaum. The sisters. All widowed.

The last shower she went to, where was it? Probably for Leah's daughter, Terry. Or was it for Eileen, her assistant at Abbott Casuals who married so late? Later than this? She laughed to herself. Not bloody likely.

CHAPTER

32

LOOK HOW MARCIA ORGANIZED. PUT HALF THIS MUCH ENERGY into herself, she'd have three jobs, six apartments, who knows what else?

It was Saturday. She had reached everyone; Marcia was relentless.

Leah had helped with the decorations. They bought ribbons and a white crepe paper umbrella just like the one she had for Marcia's own shower. Plenty of bridge chairs. Ida had almost as many bridge chairs as she had watchbands.

The only difference between today's shower and others she had attended was that no one attempted to make this a surprise. Of course not, Marcia wanted Ella to prepare the stuffed cabbage, her specialty, and the chopped liver which she made better than anyone except Guadalupe. Lupe was too busy cleaning and turning out apple pies to be asked to make chopped liver as well.

At twelve promptly the buzzer started to ring. The relatives were, as always, on time. Especially for Ella's stuffed cabbage. They knew they could count on that.

So much kissing, so much squeezing. Who was missing? The Birnbaum sisters used to be six. Now only Flossie, Helen, and Gussie. All in polka dot. Or white flowered prints, which was it? Ella couldn't remember, so much got mixed up. Charlotte came with Ruth. The babies. Only sixty-two. Everybody rose when Aunt Gussie entered. Tiny, porcelain figurine, hair brushed back, almost totally blind, but gentle and soft and looking better than some of the younger ones. She held

Sophie's arm, the two almost inseparable. Except into death, Ella prayed.

So much hugging, so much squeezing, so many tears.

"Ella, darling, such a lucky man, this fellow." She'd told them his name was Hyman. Which one of them would believe a Chip?

Even the family loved Ella Sagersdorf. She was a favored cousin, a special niece. Aunt Gussie was transferred to her side where she would cling, like a baby in a sling, for the rest of the afternoon.

They all brought presents, specially wrapped. Sadie Melman used Christmas leftovers, but the others had gone for wedding bells in white, silver, and gold. Pieces of velvet ribbon, green and red and purple (lots of cousins knew this was Ella's favorite color). They piled all the packages under the white umbrella. What can they bring me now, at this time of my life? Ella thought.

"Sit down, little bride." Hannah said. They all laughed. One of them had made it. Again. They felt the excitement, the joy mixed with envy.

"You have to open each gift and we'll save the strings and the ribbons," she was told. Cousin Mary, the neat one, the organizer, was positioned on the other side of Ella (Aunt Gussie still held to her station) to hold the paper, save the string.

Cute little gifts emerged. Soaps, paper towels, scents, honey pots, small plants, candles. What they could afford now. The decibel count was high. The voices clanged together, braced, and veered off in other directions.

When she finished opening the last gift, Ella was in tears.

"So wonderful, you're so wonderful. I'm such a lucky woman."

"Tee hee" from Cousin Esther. She was the only person Ella ever knew who actually said, or laughed, tee hee. "Ella, I've been the court stenographer, taking down what you said. *Oy,* is your face going to be red."

The ritual continues even unto death. *Vay is mir.* The things she had said as she opened the gifts. "It's such a beautiful color, it's big, it's got this funny thing on the end, look how it wiggles," and more. The way they used to do it at the showers of their (hopefully) virgin daughters. Everybody holding their sides, laughing. "That's what you'll say to your husband on the wedding night."

At her age, yet. They meant it. She looked around at them. They were all virgins again, all young girls, living through her, Ella, starting her new life. Wondering what it would be like on the wedding night. Some of it forgotten. Pain and pleasure mixed together, had they enjoyed it? Really?

She would climb into bed with Chip. In would bounce Hannah, and Sophie and Sadie, and Eva and Ruby and Helen —all of them together on her wedding night. Did they think if you didn't use it, you became a virgin again? Break the hymen, here's the bride in white.

She walked, Aunt Gussie on the arm, leading the crowd to the table, set as a buffet, the way they liked it. The best part of the celebration. Any celebration. The food. They would talk about this for days, weeks. What Ella served. How good the chopped liver was. How Sophie got heartburn from the stuffed cabbage. How Marcia, imagine, made the noodle pudding. How nice the radishes were cut up, but what were those funny things in the salad? (Bean sprouts were not de rigueur in Jewish homes). They'd sigh over the mold made with carrots inside lime jello, so pretty. Everyone would eat too many of Leah's rugelach, Charlotte's chocolate chip cookies.

Then they would remember other meals. Mary's seder, Ruth's Thanksgiving dinner, Aunt Gussie's latkes for Chanukah. Flossie's gefilte fish to break the fast on Yom Kippur, Gussie's son's bar mitzvah, each morsel of food recalled as if it were yesterday. Ella joined in. She liked this, loved the intimacy of the women's group. They had always been together. Sure, maybe ignored by the husbands. At the start they pretended. Faked it. That they didn't really like each other's company best, just the women alone. "If they'd include us, we wouldn't have this kaffeeklatsch," yet secretly rejoicing. Tsk, tsking each other, laying on the hands, comforting, patting the hair, listening, always listening, ears open to each other. Family, we're family, she used to tell Marcia and Donald. It's special. You should know your cousins. It's terrible that you aren't closer. I still talk to my cousins, my relatives. By phone. We send cards. Get better. Happy New Year. Happy Chanukah. Happy Birthday. We remember each other. Nobody forgotten. There's a cousin you can phone, write, you need help. Always come, right away. No questions asked. Each one of them.

Still beautiful to her. The wrinkles didn't matter. She remembered their faces clear, soft, and pink. All the eyes, still shiny, still alert. No dummies in our family, Ella reckoned.

And they came today. Just a bit of notice, probably broke dates, who knows what, to come, to give Ella a good send-off. Let them take out their pictures. Everybody look at each other's. Oooh for the grandchildren, cluck for the grown sons and daughters. Listen in awe at the parade of fellowships, degrees bestowed upon this young Jewry. Aunt Gussie nodding as Ella recited the litany of success in her ear. As it should be, Aunt Gussie said. As it should be. Learn, learn, it's good for you. Eat, eat, Aunt Gussie had also said.

She told Chip to come about three. They all had to meet him. "We're just getting married in front of the rabbi, no ceremony, so he'll drop in and say hello."

And he came, the king. And they kvelled for her, for their own Ella. Such a prize, such a nice man, kind eyes, firm handshake. God willing, he's healthy. If not, hope he leaves her well provided. Friendly, and he's not even from New York. Accepted. The real ceremony was over.

CHAPTER

33

MARCIA HAD BEEN VERY SECRETIVE FOR THE PAST SEVERAL days. Silent around the apartment, creeping quietly out and returning the same way. Ella confided to Leah that she was worried.

"If she's looking for a job, Leah, wouldn't she just tell me that she's going out on interviews, something like that? It's no secret. In fact, she'd be proud."

"That's true," her friend agreed.

"So what does it mean if she says nothing, just nods, comes like a mouse, goes like a cat? It's not my Marcia."

"Do you know anyone she knows? You could call and sort of feel around, you know?"

"I know a few." Lois and Geraldine from the women's group. Oh, oh, Carole? No, not for Marcia. "Hmmm. Tony Dappolita."

"Tony Whoozis?"

"Dappolita. Adonis. Marcia is attracted to him. Or was. I don't know if he's still in Miami. He was a boyfriend of hers. A ski instructor. Or so they tell me."

"Ella, she wouldn't go with him, you know your Marcia."

Did she know her Marcia? How do you know somebody you haven't lived with for so many years? Of course, they'd been in touch, but it was hearing what Marcia wanted to tell, not observing firsthand. Ella didn't meet any of her boyfriends after the divorce. It wasn't the way it used to be: the teen years. The parade of tall, short, cheerful, dour, clear-eyed, pimpled-skin young men coming to shake hands with the mama and the papa before they squired the jewel to the ball, saying a few innocuous words (Ella never remembered holding an interesting conversation with any of Marcia's dates. On the other hand, Donald had wonderful girlfriends, all bright and energetic, very like Holly in fact—he ran true to form) and departing. Quickly forgotten. Yes, but she saw them, they had identities. Who approved the men after Stanley, who looked them over? Ella had always felt she'd be able to pick the mass murderer out of that adolescent bunch and stop him at the door. Except that none of them ever looked virile enough to be a mass murderer. (How many Jewish mass murderers were there anyway, how many Jewish rapists, muggers?) But now? Who could tell what a Tony Dappolita would do? Maybe white slavery. Come on, Ella, where will he sell a forty-year-old divorcée? Maybe Uganda, Mali, Goa. Places like that, they'd love a nice white woman from America.

"This will be the death of me, Leah. When she lived in New York I was out of touch, I just assumed everything was okay. Look how wrong I was then."

"What are you worrying about? She is fine. Just give the kids some time."

It was obscene. The kids. Each one of *them*, by God, has children. Real ones.

"We don't have so much time, Leah. The wedding is the fifteenth and neither one of them has made a move. Has Donald talked to you about making that call to Sidney George?"

"Negative."

"Leah, you have to help me. Pick me up at nine tomorrow. Wait downstairs in the car, don't come up."

"What for, where are we going?"

"You drive, I'll direct. See you bright and early."

She had asked Leah to park across the street. She slipped

out the door, calling a goodbye at Donald's sleeping form. Marcia was in the bathroom, getting ready, and Ella wanted to be in Leah's car when she came downstairs.

There she was, wonderful Leah.

"I made some egg salad sandwiches." Ella indicated the shopping bag. This might take a full day, who knew?

"I got some Danish to go with the coffee. They're in the white bag next to the thermos."

"I'll just have a little nibble, I should calm my nerves." Ella flung herself at the bag lying on the back seat.

"Hey, look at that Rolls Royce just pulling into your driveway. Boy, is that a beautiful car. I could feel like a queen in one of those. It's just not an Irving car, you know what I mean? An Irving car is a Cadillac, a Buick, you understand, Ella? Terry's husband is a Sting Ray, Donald is a Volkswagen. Chip is a Volvo. A little different in Walla Walla, but just not enough chutzpah for a Rolls. Who drives one in your building?"

"Nobody I ever saw." Ella watched the driver get out, an unfamiliar-looking and undistinguished man, tall and gray. He went inside the building.

"Look, there's Ida on her terrace. Does she have breakfast out there every day?" Leah turned to Ella.

"Probably. And in flowered chintz, I'm sure." She kept her eyes on the door, didn't want to lose Marcia leaving the building.

"Leah, Leah, there she is with the man from the Rolls!" Alternately pointing and stabbing Leah with the same finger.

"Is that the Italian fellow?" Leah asked.

"No, no, Tony is younger. I don't know this one. Fix, rev, do whatever you have to do to the motor so we don't get started too slow. Isn't a Rolls a fast car?"

"It's not fast, it's just expensive. Don't worry about my car. We'll follow them. How many Rollses are around this morning? Sweetheart, relax. I've been watching the goddamn

TV shows for so long I got the procedure down pat."

So had Ella. She realized that it was true. Here they were, totally prepared to follow that car, to dog the Rolls down any mean street, to stalk the suspects. Only problem is that we aren't wired into the precinct, Ella thought. If we lose them, we lose them.

It wasn't difficult. Obviously, the tall, gray man and Marcia were in no hurry to get to their destination.

"Where do you suppose they're going, Leah? Maybe somebody else rented the car. Maybe Tony Dappolita doesn't want to be seen near my house, so he sent one of his . . . hoods."

"I thought he was a ski instructor?"

"That's what they always say. I can see through his disguise."

The Rolls was slowing in front of a very large, pink stucco house. The tall, gray man exited and ran to open the door for Marcia.

"Subservient. See that." Leah was enjoying this caper. "I think he's just the fetcher, the real person is inside that stucco house."

"How are we going to find out who lives there?"

"Marcia would spot you in a minute, Ella. I'll stick on this hat and see what name is on the doorbell. Give me your sunglasses in case she walks out the door."

Ella watched Leah walk, stealthily, like a trained sleuth, to the bell. She opened her purse and wrote swiftly.

"This is *not* an Italian name," Leah said as she slid back into the car. "Garcia Gomez." Said it with a question mark. Ella remembered years ago, when Marcia was seventeen, walking into Marcia's bedroom, saying in that same questioning way, "Someone named Patrick Donovan is on the phone." For you, she had wanted to add: what kind of name is that?

"Garcia Gomez," Ella said. "He has two last names. Like Sidney George, he has two first names. We could match them up. Sidney Garcia. George Gomez. What do you call this man, Garcia?"

"Look, Ella, this could be perfectly legitimate. Someone could have told her about a job, maybe governess for this family."

"She's a little old for Jane Eyre, Leah. And don't try to tell me she's catering a wedding."

"Remember Terry's wedding? My sister hired the caterer. I went into the kitchen and who's there? Mr. Slassinger, the piano teacher. A caterer. Made more money that way and his ulcers disappeared." She laughed.

"Are you trying to tell me that Garcia Gomez is Mr. Slassinger?" Ella was confused.

"I'm just trying to cheer you up."

"Well, you're not succeeding. What if she stays here all day? How will we know what she did and who this Gomez is?"

"Do you know anyone in this neighborhood?"

"No, but I just thought of something. Give me a pad."

Found one in the glove compartment. "What are you going to do?"

"Don't worry, I'll think of something. Now listen, if Marcia leaves while I'm gone, you follow her in the car. If I see you're not parked, I'll know you're on the tail. I'll get to a phone booth and wait there."

"How will I know what phone booth you're in?"

"Leah, don't be stupid, you won't. God. I'll call your house. Is Irving home?" Leah nodded. "I'll call Irving and when you get set—but don't go to a phone booth where you can't watch Marcia—when you get set call Irving and tell him exactly where you are. I'll call a cab and come to you."

"And if she leaves that place and I follow, what will you do?"

"The same thing. You'll call Irving again. Tell him. And let's hope he doesn't have to pee. Stick by the phone, Irv, be a good soldier." They giggled.

"Leah, at all costs, keep your eye on Marcia. Don't lose her." She collected the notebook, put it in the big purse, checked to be sure she had a pen. "Wait."

"What else?" Leah asked her.

"I'll take one of the egg salad sandwiches."

CHAPTER

34

THIS NAME WASN'T SPANISH. LOCATELLI. A GOOD ITALIAN name. Guess this wasn't your big Jewish neighborhood. Leave it to Marcia to show her mother the sights, how the other world lives. She pressed the doorbell, big smile ready.

The woman who answered the door was not a real blonde. She had light hair, yes, but very dark roots. Her eyebrows were black, as were the pencil lines around the eyes themselves. The mascara had been applied with a paint roller; no brush could do a job like that. She wore a two-piece number that in Ella's day had been called sharkskin. It was low cut, very. Revealing two pink melons, overripe.

"Yeah, what can I do for you?"

Not your cultured British voice. This was New York, possibly Brooklyn, transplanted. The sunshine had not improved the quality.

"I'm Sybil Churchill, dear." Getting a lot mileage out of that dame, Ella girl, but a Jewish name would sit like a stale bagel in this atmosphere. "I'm taking a poll. And I wondered if you might be able to spare a few minutes."

Locatelli looked her over. Didn't seem a dangerous woman, Ella didn't, little old lady, couldn't-hurt-a-fly type. "Sure, the kids are in school, I don't have a thing to do. The maid cleans, you know. My husband won't let me lift a finger."

To do what? Ella thought.

Locatelli gestured, and Ella followed her inside. She had a good maid indeed. The place was spotless. You could eat off the you know what. A lot of glass, chrome, and gold thread.

Obviously, Mrs. Locatelli liked a little bit of everything and she had assembled it all in the living room. Ella noticed wicker chairs off in one corner, a Queen Anne chair in another, a sectional couch done up in ruby red velvet, armless chairs, coffee tables (several), and many pictures of flowers on the walls. Insulting the fireplace was one of the most grotesque Madonna and child reproductions Ella had ever seen. Probably done with numbers by Mrs. Locatelli herself.

"Call me Angie," the latter said, "and I'll call you Sybil. I hate to be formal, you know? When Joey has parties, everybody is so stiff, and not from booze, honey." She giggled.

"Well, it sounds like you have a lot of parties and a lot of fun, doesn't it?"

"Yeah, it's okay, I can't complain. My Joey likes to dance and we go out maybe three times a week. When he's in town, anyway. Rest of the time he travels. I'm from Brooklyn, where you from?"

Bullseye, Ella thought. "I'm from Walla Walla, Washington. It's very far away, dear, on the West Coast, and I don't know anybody from New York." Better play it safe.

"So what kinda poll you taking?"

Ella thought fast. "We're moving into a new religious age. With Carter as president, we're getting down to your basic values again. You understand, dear, like honor thy father and thy mother." Something off key there, Ella decided. "Or love thy neighbor," she added hastily.

"Yeah," Angie said. "And that's a good thing. My parents are wonderful people and I honor them. I miss them a lot." Wiping a tear away.

"And that's the point of the poll. Love thy neighbors. We wonder how many people really *know* their neighbors. Who lives on each side of you, who's across the street, things like that."

"Hey, that's really interesting. Can you tell me how it's going?"

"Well, dear, very few people score well. They don't even

know the people next door, isn't that awful? But you know, Angie," she leaned forward and opened her purse, "I have a strong feeling that you're not like that. I have a feeling you really do know your neighbors."

"Well, I'm always home, not like Joey. So I guess I do. I'm also real friendly." Ella was in luck. What if she'd picked the house on the other side of Garcia Gomez and they turned out to be real prunes?

"Who lives to the right side of you?" Ella asked it simply, pencil poised over the pad.

"Let me tell you about the people on the other side first," Angie perked. *Oy vay*, Ella thought, no way to get out of this.

"The Shaws. Amazing. He's a much older man and very rich. She's young, like my age. And she's got five kids."

"That's wonderful, dear, you really know those people. Now to the ones on the other. . . ."

"Wait till you hear how *well* I know them." Angie was not to be put off. "He's got another wife on the other side of town, a woman like your age, Sybil, and *they* have five children and there are grandchildren too. And he's not really married to the one next door, Betty is her name. She's got a lot of money from her father. And she doesn't care that they're not married. She told me so. She'll get him eventually because his other wife is dying of cancer." Angie was beaming. "So whadda ya think?"

"You really do know them. Goodness. But what about the other side?"

"Real winners." Obviously no love lost here. "I don't know them *socially* for obvious reasons. But I've talked to them, both of them."

"Oh, then it is a family, may I put that down?"

"Yeah, a man and his wife. He's Cuban, see, and she's American. Flaky."

"Flaky?" Ella was puzzled.

"You know, when people do strange things, that's what

you call flaky. And these people are the flakiest. You should
see them, wow!"

Ella sat forward. "Dear, could you be a little more specific?"

"I can see them from my bedroom window. They sit and
talk and walk around in the . . . nude. Even in the day-
time, isn't that disgusting?" Her melons quivered in their
sharkskin blanket.

"Oh, yes," Ella agreed.

"They swim, they stand around on the lawn. They even
invited me to come over once but I refused. Joey would kill
me."

Where did Marcia meet these people? Why is she doing
this? Orgies in the nude? Ella was struggling with it, it was
worse than she had dreamed.

What was Angie asking? "Is this poll going to be pub-
lished?"

"Oh, no, dear, just the results, to see how many people
know their neighbors. And you do, Angie. You're the best so
far."

"You wanna cup cawfee?"

"No, dear, I have to be running. To make the rounds. I
really want to thank you. Very much." She got up and slowly
made her way to the door. Miserably.

When she got outside, Leah's car wasn't in sight. Starsky
must be on the tail. Had to find a telephone. Call Irving. The
excitement almost washed away the shame of what she'd just
heard. Almost. Turning a corner she found a gas station with
a phone.

"Irving?"

"Ella, what is going on? Why is Leah in one place and you
in the other?"

"I'll tell you later, Irv. Where is she?"

He gave her the address. She wrote it down in the notebook.
Like Hutch would do. She forgot to say goodbye. What was
happening to her Marcia? Some evil genius had taken control

of her mind. Making her walk around naked and maybe trying to recruit her as a prostitute. Train her in a massage parlor. Who knew? She dialed a cab company and waited.

The cab arrived instantly. "Hey, lady, I was just gassing up here when you called. Funny, heh?"

Let this joker enjoy himself. She didn't feel like laughing. She gave him the address.

Maybe she and Leah could break in, sort of smash open the door and make a citizen's arrest. She spotted Leah's car. "Here it is, driver. Just let me off here."

"Leah!" Ella opened the door and plopped down. "I don't know whether I'll live through this."

"You'll live, you'll live. Let's eat the egg salad sandwiches now and get some strength."

"Okay." Ella thought it was a good idea. She looked across at the house they were parked near. It seemed dignified and quiet. "And when we finish eating, we'll storm the place."

"How storm?" Leah had to know practicalities.

"We'll push in the door and take them all by surprise and I'll drag Marcia out. Then we'll call the police and break up this ring. White slavers, momzers."

"It sounds dangerous. What if they have a gun?"

"Why would they have a gun?"

"To kill people who break down the doors and storm in."

"Okay," Ella said, "so we'll just amble in, like we're . . . customers. Do they have men working in these places too?"

"I guess so." Leah didn't seem too sure.

"Let's case the joint first, and then we'll decide. By the way, where is the Rolls?"

"Oh, that was strange, Ella. I forgot to tell you. A woman came out with her. Not the tall man. Marcia's age. She dropped her here and, Ella, she kissed her goodbye."

"Nu? So don't I kiss you goodbye? What's the big deal? Still—let's get ourselves inside in a hurry."

It was a very small white house with a very discreet sign and a funny name. Ella couldn't pronounce it. They opened the door slowly. There were other doors inside, apartment-like. That was just a disguise, she was sure. They clung to-gether, Nancy Drew and her pal, and edged down the cor-ridor.

There was a sign over the door to Apartment 5. Ella put her hand on the knob. It turned. She opened the door slowly. They eased in.

It was very quiet. Pretty Japanese screens blocked the view at one side of the room. Ella pulled Leah after her. She peered around a screen.

There, lying naked on the floor, was Marcia. Even lying on her stomach, Ella recognized her. And kneeling over her, oh obscene sight, was this Oriental man and his hands were all over her.

The man seemed to sense their presence without looking around. "Just a minute, prease. Wait on other side screen. I be right there."

The shock made them obey. Marcia, Ella noticed, did not move at all from her position.

The man beckoned them into a small room off to one side. "We speak softly. Not to disturb mood, prease. You have appointment?"

What kind of sex scene was this? Ella wondered. He kept his clothes on, hers were off. Is that what they call kinky sex, he just open his. . . . ? She didn't want to think about it. "We'd like one, please."

"Tomorrow morning, ten. Name, prease?" He wrote it carefully. Spelling Sybil Churchill correctly without help.

Starsky and Hutch left quickly, running to Leah's car.

"Ella, what's going on?"

"Do I know? She was naked, that I know. What did it look like she was doing? I've got to face her, Leah. I've got to talk to her. She's in real trouble and she needs me now. And I've been too busy to notice."

"You want to tail her some more? Do you know enough?

"I suppose. Oh, wait." Ella saw the familiar figure at the

door of the little white house. Waiting, patiently. Ella could tell that. Maybe, at last, Tony Dappolita, the engineer of this destruction, would emerge. No, a cab pulled up.

"Leah, don't lose her. Quick." Ella commanded and Leah pulled out in pursuit. Now. We'll have the truth at last.

Or would they? Leah followed the cab smack into the driveway of Bimini Towers. Marcia was getting out and glanced casually toward them.

"Leah, Mom," she said. "What a pleasant coincidence."

CHAPTER

35

"WHAT DID YOU DO THIS MORNING, DARLING?" BAD OPENING. Wasn't giving her any room.

"Not much, Ma."

"Leah and I went for a drive, a little shopping, and I'm exhausted, can you believe it?" Change the tone. Make her more comfortable. Sideways.

"Are you feeling okay, dear? You've been so quiet lately. Not even fighting with Donald." She threw in a light laugh. Disarming.

"Actually, Mom, new things have been happening. I'm beginning to find my true self. And when I do, I know everything will be fine."

What true self? This isn't Marcia? So who is? "How are you doing it, dear? Meditation?"

Marcia looked startled. "Actually, in a way we, I mean I, am into meditation. And other things."

"Other things? You seeing a therapist?"

"Ma, if I were seeing a doctor you'd be paying for it, right? So you know it's not a doctor I'm seeing."

"Then what are you doing? You don't have to tell me if you don't want to. After all, you're a grown person. . . ."

"Ma, I'll tell you before you drop of curiosity."

Ella felt sanguine. Sanguine? The vocabulary word. Good. Secure in knowledge that. Let her try to lie to me now, I'll catch her.

"Remember Joslyn Feinstein?"

Already the lie. Who cared about some old friend from

Syracuse? Of course she remembered Joslyn. She'd spent enough weekends at the apartment. "So?"

"Joslyn moved to California with her first husband. And she became a therapist out there, into different training techniques. Anyway, she had a great romance with this Cuban, a businessman, rich, and she divorced her husband and married Raul."

"Who's Raul?" A new twist to the story.

"Her husband. Raul Garcia Gomez." Oh ho, that explained the name; and the kiss in the car. Maybe. "She met him at a session in California. . . ."

"Marcia, what's a session?"

"Well, she was a group leader in this therapy training. Nude encounter groups."

"Nude?" Ella couldn't believe it. Groups? *Organized* naked?

"It's a way of discovering yourself, Ma. It peels off the false layers. Puts you in touch with other people, men and women. And not in a sexual way."

How can it not be sexual if you touch? Ella was aghast. You touch a naked body, it's sexual. She hadn't a doubt on that score.

"Joslyn has been letting me come for free. She's really a doll. She even sends her husband to pick me up." So the tall gray man was Raul Garcia Gomez.

"And Jos treated me to something equally wonderful today —a Shiatsu massage."

The pieces were falling into place. "So that's all? Just that?"

"You just don't understand new ways, Mother." The word "Mother" meant trouble. An attack, the whole panzer division was coming. Ella braced herself.

"The way to find oneself, to get in touch with oneself, is by shedding old ways. Free your body, emerge into the sunlight, cleansed, unscathed."

Bullshit. For this Phil spent all that money on college? Shiatsu, that was the word on the door?

"Joslyn is trying to help me. She's letting me attend these sessions and eventually I might be able to become an assistant, which would pay back what I owe now. See, Mom, it's a slow process, but Jos insists that it is worth the time. When I emerge it will be with strength, with a purpose. . . ."

"What bull!" Hello? Donald was listening? "Jesus, what nonsense," he grimaced. Who knew he was in the apartment at all? In the bathroom, she supposed. Hers, for Chrissakes?

"It's *not* nonsense. It's very helpful," Marcia repeated.

"Bull, I live in California. They have a new therapy birthing every week. It's like a contest. Today's panacea is. . . ."

"All I can tell you is that this is working for me. I'm sure it wouldn't work on your brilliant mind."

"Marcia, Donald, this is serious. Don't poke fun at her, Donald, and don't put him down, Marcia. Let's see what the prospects are."

"She can write a book called *The Naked Neurotic Meets the Shiatsu Masseuse.* . . ."

"Shut up, you asshole. Every time I feel better, I have to come back here and face your insults."

"Quiet. Let's keep the voices down." At least try, Ella thought.

"I don't want to talk to him," and Marcia flew into the second bedroom and shut the door. Not gently. Ella was expecting a shower of plaster any day.

"Ella, you can't let her get away with this kind of nonsense, can you? You have to talk to her."

"I let you both get away with lots of nonsense all your life, why should I change now? I'm going to lie down a little."

She started to walk toward her room but changed her mind.

"Donnie, anything happening with the college?" Casual question, unrushed.

"You are relentless, Ella. Yes, I went to see the head of the department. Which one of your friends is that crazy Churchill woman? She sounds like a real cluck. Made up a pack of lies about me. Downright embarrassing. I hope I fixed it. I've got another meeting with him when I get my slides. Oh, and by the way, I called Holly and found you'd already asked for them. Right on the ball, Ella. You'll be glad to know they're in the mail." He sneered.

"I am glad. Did your meeting go well? What's he like?"

"An ass, but what can you expect? Don't worry, I was so nice butter was melting."

"Good. So what's the chance of a job there?"

"Pretty good. I have to see if I want one. In fact, there may be an opening for next month. Somebody in the department is sick."

What does he have to think about? The two of them, discovering their bodies and their minds. Forty-some-odd years and neither of them was aware of a head before. And *her* mind? Ella's? *That* shouldn't be allowed a little peace?

"Ella, I know this isn't easy for you. I'm trying. I don't know what the hell *she's* doing besides playing the princess, but I've been at least doing the portraits and getting paid. I haven't asked you for money these last few days, have I?"

No, it was true, he hadn't. But still, but still. . . .

"You know, Donald, the wedding is for the fifteenth. And then Chip comes here. I would like to know you and Marcia were at least beginning to start your new lives."

"I'm aware of it, Ella. I'm trying. Maybe you can get Marcia a job as a receptionist to a Jewish doctor who will leave his present wife to marry her."

"That's really mean."

"So what happened to the women's group? I thought you were making her over? Maybe you can turn her into a lesbian and she can move in with Carole Cavalcanti."

"Shut up. You're not so perfect, Donald. Maybe you hadn't noticed. . . ."

"I know that, but I don't float around like a goddamn shadow. She's got no guts."

The door was flung open. "I've got guts, you son of a bitch. I've got more guts than you. Living off your wife, not doing a lick of work, you fucking genius. Talking art, pretending you're so special, better than me."

"Hallelujah, we got a rise out of her. She's not dead after all."

"Marcia, into your room. Donald into, into . . . go take a walk." Could she really live through this?

She rested on her bed for about half an hour. The apartment was quiet. Donald did go out, then. She went into the bathroom, threw some drops of water into her eyes, brushed her hair and looked into Marcia's room. Marcia was lying there on the floor. Meditating, Ella supposed.

"Sweetheart, I'm worried about you. I thought being with Lois, Geraldine, and the others would help you. You know, to stand on your own, but. . . ."

"Ma, they have helped me. You can't expect me to change overnight. Can I stand on my own two feet if I can't afford to? I have to think about the various possibilities for me. Which is the reason I went to Joslyn's group."

"I don't understand—"

"Ma, wait. Tony Dappolita made me an offer. Don't look at me that way. It's a business proposition. There's a new resort opening in Venezuela. Tony wants to hire me to act as hostess/manager for the lodge. Greet the guests, make sure the books are right, no cheating. Its . . ."

"You'd have to live with him? In a country where they don't speak English yet?"

"It would not be a sexual arrangement. And some of the money would come from Raul, Joslyn's husband. And others. Tony just wants to have someone he trusts watching the collections, and he does trust me. I am an honorable person, Ma."

"I know that. That's not the problem. What if something happens to you when you're there? Who will take care of you?"

"That's what I need to think about, Ma. Now you see why

I've been so nervous lately. I know I've been bothering you. But I have to see if this feels right for me. If it does, I'd take off and do it. For a while, anyway, what have I got to lose?"

Venezuela? Who goes there? Nobody Ella knew. Okay, when Donald lived in Mexico, it was over the border, you could even go by car. Venezuela, you could only fly there. Was it one of the countries with revolutions? With kidnappings? Had she pushed Marcia to this choice?

"Marcia, if I weren't marrying Chip when I am, would you have considered this offer?"

"It has nothing to do with your marriage. Of course I would have considered it. I have to get out on my own, Ma, it really is time. I know that. I don't do it well, but I do think about it. And you have helped me, you really have."

"But so far away? I think I'd prefer the offer from that old lecher, you know, giving you an apartment. At least you'd be right here."

Marcia laughed. "I don't think that would work at all. Just think of this as temporary anyway. I will pursue it with Tony. I don't know why you've taken such a dislike to him, he's not a bad guy. And he'd be a very loyal friend. After all, he needs an honest sidekick."

"When will you know for sure?"

"By the fourteenth or the fifteenth."

"A wedding present. Your happiness—" She couldn't stop the tears. She loved her children, wanted them to be perfect jewels. So many flaws they had. But it didn't diminish the love, the emotion that she carried with her.

Venezuela. Caracas. Aruba. On second thought, didn't Leah and Irving go on a cruise there? Maybe she and Chip could plan one. Visit Marcia. Have a holiday. Two wonderful months in downtown Venezuela. Skiing, group sex for everyone over sixty-five. Continental breakfast and Latin swinging. Olé.

CHAPTER

36

ON THE BOAT WERE ALICE FAYE, DON AMECHE, BETTY Grable, and Cesar Romero. Carmen Miranda looked suspiciously like Shirley Mittelman. All of them, the whole she-bang, were going to Venezuela. Betty stood up and sang a song about the need to go to Caracas where the rum comes from or where you shake the maracas. In Caracas.

They were all staying at the Marcia Adelson Lodge and Motor Court, featuring Tony Dappolita on the ski slopes. The boat pulled in and streamers of crepe paper covered Ella. As she looked at her face in the large gilt hand mirror, Carole Lombard's face smiled back at her. She put a rose in her teeth.

Claude Rains was at the dock to greet the boat. Customs official extraordinaire, of course. A big yellow bus waited to take them to the Lodge. In the front of it Benny Goodman and his band were playing. In the rear, Xavier Cugat waited to warm up. They formed a conga line, Alice Faye in the lead, and snaked onto the bus. Ella was having a ball.

José Gonzalez, the driver, spoke a pidgin Spanish. "Call me Joe," he told them. Betty Grable cuddled with Cesar Romero. Alice Faye sang "Hello, Venezuela, Hello." The bus stopped to pick up Tyrone Power, local bullfighter and son of the biggest landowner in Caracas, Leo Carillo. He and Alice Faye traded glances. They were hopelessly in love. Ella knew *her* chance would come.

They pulled up before a magnificent ski lodge. Pine trees, Swiss chalets, where Bing Crosby was crooning "White Christmas." Inside, a glowing fire roared in the fireplace, stoked by a tall, dark-haired man who kept his back to the arrivals. Behind the desk stood Marcia, with Gale Sondergaard at her side, taking names and assigning rooms. Greta Garbo, swathed in furs, was smoking a very long cigarette in the corner. Frederic March was warming her feet, rubbing them between his palms.

Ella was shown into a large room with a canopied bed and a view of the mountains, breathtaking. Very much like Switzerland.

The maid, Lupe Velez, entered. Sounds of an argument came from the next room. Ella put her ear against the wall. She could hear the voice of Helmut Dantine shouting and the voice of Curt Jurgens shouting back. You fool, we must act tonight, or incur the wrath of the Führer.

There was a knock on Ella's door. It was Marcia. Madame, Ella was told, I recognize you as a woman of the world, one I can trust. There are Nazis in this hotel and they are trying to kill us and take over. Sidney Greenstreet told them who I was and they are going to send me back to Germany. Charles Boyer is trying to aid me. He is on the shortwave radio to Lloyd Nolan in Washington. Will you help us?

Ella followed her down a long corridor to a big white room. In one corner sat José Iturbi at the white piano. Ginger Rogers and Fred Astaire were dancing the Continental. Ella could see Louis Hayward sitting in a small room off to the right. He was writing a letter to the world; the country was in danger. Paul Muni, the president of Venezuela, entered at that moment. He told Ella that Bette Davis and Brian Ahearn were going to take him to a safe place. He would not return until the church bells rang in the village square once again. Errol Flynn was preparing to lead Norwegian paratroopers into the city and perhaps he would save them.

The door was flung open. Marcia ran toward it, but it was too late. Claude Rains had his gun pointed at Tony Dappolita. Marcia screamed. Wicked Claude Rains was really a tool of the Nazis. They heard the whistle in the distance. Humphrey Bogart tootling the *Marseillaise*. Move aside, he told Claude Rains, while I comfort the dames.

Ella's heart began to flutter as she glanced into the eyes of the man who entered behind Bogart. It was Clark Gable! Handsomer than handsome. Bogey told him to take care of Ella. She followed after him with great anticipation. Marcia was whimpering. Gable beckoned. Carmen Miranda, Alice Faye, and Betty Grable were now singing an old Andrews Sisters number. Gable still beckoned. They were beginning to feel the first tremors of an earthquake. Marcia still whimpered. Gable still beckoned. You can't leave me, Madame, Marcia was calling. Gable, beckoning, smiled.

Grow up, kid, Ella mouthed over her shoulder. Can't you see I'm busy?

Fadeout.

CHAPTER
37

"MARCIA, WOULD IT BE A TERRIBLE THING IF I WENT TO this group with you? I mean at Joslyn's."

"It might be difficult for you, Ma. People do take off their clothes."

"Does a person have to? Supposing a person wants to wear something light? Or if a person gets chilly?"

Marcia nodded. "Ma, I know you always liked to taste new treats, and I suppose I could persuade Jos to let you come. I just hope you won't prove to be a disruptive element."

Ella was perplexed. "I'm very cooperative. Didn't the women in the other group like me? I don't understand."

They decided it would be best to take a cab. Perhaps Raul or someone else in the group could bring them home. But Ella didn't want anyone to know where they were going.

Ella couldn't help the feeling that butterflies were nesting in her stomach. There was no way to treat this calmly. It was important to Marcia and Ella was determined not to mess it up.

As the cab pulled up in front of the door, Angie Locatelli bounced out of her own house. Panic button. Ella upended her purse onto the floor of the cab. "Go in without me, dear, I'll just collect my things." Watching until pink sharkskin crossed the street and got into what must be her very own Cadillac. Ella rushed after Marcia.

Joslyn was at the door. Wearing clothes.

"Hi, Marcia said you were anxious to come. And we're pleased you wanted to join us. Come out back into the garden."

No halfway mark. Jump right in. Adam and Eve probably out there chomping on McIntosh apples. Ella padded after Joslyn, over the carpets and into the woods.

"Would you like to leave your shoes here?" Joslyn asked.

Seemed safe. And nonthreatening. "Sure." She unhooked the sandals, noted the purses resting there as well, and extracted her sunglasses. Something to hide behind. A deep breath, and Ella walked with determination to the pool.

A gulp thereafter. In the pool. She knew those people were not wearing bathing suits. Not on your life. She could see the nipples of the women. Where was Marcia? She sat down in a lounge chair by the side of the pool and removed her light jacket. She was wearing a sleeveless blouse. That seemed brief enough. Glanced up to spy Joslyn removing her dress. Over the head it went. No panties, no bra. Just flesh. Skinny, not very sexy at all. Very sparse pubic hair. Itsy bitsy titties. Joslyn saw Ella looking and waved at her. At that moment a very hairy and very naked man exited the pool. He was walking over to Ella.

Hand outstretched. "I'm Raul Garcia Gomez. You're Marcia's mother. Welcome to our group."

She concentrated on a mole near his right shoulder. "It's a pleasure to be here. My daughter has told me so much about you."

Another man appeared. Blond and equally naked. Such a long, skinny penis he had. *Vay is mir.* Almost to the knees. Her Marcia in the middle of this?

Raul drew him over. "Giorgio, meet Ella. This is Marcia's mother."

Radiant smile. When Ella lifted her eyes, the white teeth blinded her. "Let me sit here and explain some of this, darling." He wiggled into the lounge next to her, draping that penis over his thigh, ever so gently. The butterflies in her stomach had reproduced and there were hundreds of them fluttering about. *Oy.*

"First let me tell you that I adore men. I'm outrageously gay. Outrageously. And what I love best after beautiful men are mothers. Like you, dear. You're such a pretty one." He leaned forward to pat her cheek. The thing on the thigh slithered along with him.

"How long are you going naked? I mean you just do it here, right?"

"Oh, my goodness, no. I'm the sweetheart of Fire Island. Cherry Grove. I parade up and down the beach. Eternally. The group here is teaching me how to live with myself. How to be comfortable with what I am. It really has done a lot for me. I seem to manage to keep my clothes on in most other places." He giggled.

"I heard of Fire Island. I'm from New York too, you know. But I don't take my clothes off."

"Now, now, don't be defensive, dear."

A large, big-breasted, older woman was passing. "It's Harriet. Darling, come over," Fire Island called.

Layers of barest flesh rumbled to Ella's side. "I'm Harriet and I'm glad you could come. Maybe I can persuade you to join us for a swim. Without your clothes, of course."

Fortunately, at that moment, there came Marcia. Draped in a towel. Decorously draped too, thank goodness. "I'd really rather relax here for a while," Ella managed to Harriet. "Until I get some idea of what you're doing."

"Going back to the womb," Harriet told her. "Feeling good."

She saw Marcia walk to the side of the pool and sit down. Oops! Not two seconds later she had slithered out of the towel and was into the pool. Fire Island bounded up, dragging his penis along with him. Ping, he was in also.

This was going to save her daughter? Find her a job? Big deal, you went into the water with no clothes on. Years ago they called it skinny dipping. That's someone's idea of happiness?

Suddenly Harriet's voice was booming. "Everybody, float now! Drop your excess baggage into the water. Let it sink. Hang loose. Drink in the sunbeams. Smile at the forces around you."

This was ridiculous, the excess baggage school of therapy. She'd have to get Marcia back to the women's group immediately.

"Marcia, you're looking more beautiful every day." Harriet, again. "That's because you're thinking beautiful. Stay with it."

Ella looked across. Marcia's hair was wet and clinging, personally Ella thought she looked terrible. Let Marcia blow dry her hair, then Harriet could talk.

Wearily, Ella pulled herself out of the chair, strolled into the house. Discovered the den with a color television.

When Marcia found her, she was asleep on the couch in front of *Another World*.

"If God wanted us to go naked," Ella said as they left the house, "would He have let one of His children discover drip dry?"

CHAPTER

38

THE PHONE WOKE HER. IT WAS CHIP.

"Thank God we're getting married," Chip said. "I've seen so little of you lately."

"I know," she agreed. "I've been busy with Donald and Marcia. I've really missed you." She reminded herself not to tell him too much. He might have *some* illusions left about the younger Sagersdorfs.

"Ella dear, the trip to Israel will have to be postponed. They just couldn't make all the arrangements in so short a time. So what do you say we take our honeymoon at Passover and celebrate it in Israel then?"

"A wonderful idea, Chip. Why do we have to go away now?" Why? To get away from her own children, that's why.

"Everything is working out very well. Marcia will probably have a job in Venezuela and leave right after the wedding, and Donald is making some money on the portraits and his job with the art department will start in a month."

"Ella, I'm so pleased. You've really worked it out. They were in a mess when they first came down here. You fixed everything."

"Sweetie, I'm touched. But they did it themselves. I was just here if they needed me." What a lie. So no honeymoon. So out by the night of the fifteenth. If nothing happened by then, she'd send them to Chip's apartment. Maybe Donald could stay there until he found a place, and Marcia, maybe Lois would have room (Ella could pay her, it wouldn't be too

expensive) until she left for Venezuela. She was feeling better.
The phone rang again.

"Mom, it's Holly."

Holly? "Darling, how are you? What is it? There's nothing
wrong?"

"Listen, I'm fine. And I'm in Miami. I don't want you to
say anything to Donald, though. This is business and I'm only
going to be here for two days."

"Who's with the kids?" Ella hated herself for asking the
question. So unnecessary, would Holly just abandon them?
But the grandmother must be sure.

"The Israeli student who lives with us. Didn't I write you
about Tami? She's wonderful and the girls adore her. Frankly,
she's more capable than I am. So don't worry, dear."

"What business do you have here?"

"Some fantastic fabrics, for a special project. It came up on
a moment's notice."

"Darling, do you have time to come and see us?"

"Us? No, Mom, just you. And I don't want you to stage
one of your dramas. It will be tête-à-tête. And let's make it
neutral ground. How about you meet me at my hotel? As you'd
expect, in the grand Jewish tradition I'm at the Fontainebleau. Can you make it now?"

"I'll take a cab."

"I'm waiting." Kisses into the telephone.

Holly was waiting for Ella in the lobby. Ella hugged her.

"Look at you, so beautiful, always."

"Oh, Mom, not so beautiful. Just in shape, busy, loving
what I do. Only problem in my life is your son. Let's go sit
by the pool and talk about it."

They faced each other, two businesswomen discussing the
merchandise.

"Damaged goods, that's what I returned to you, Mom.
Damaged goods." How could Holly look so cheerful about
such a serious problem?

"What damage? He drinks a lot, maybe, and he doesn't seem to have any goals, but what damage? He isn't crippled, or anything like that."

"Mom, he doesn't limp, if that's what you mean. But his head is a mess. You have to admit that, don't you?"

Ella paused. She wanted to think this out carefully. "Holly," and she pulled her hand into her own sweating palm. "He really seems to be trying so hard. I think he's determined to change. You know, he's doing some portraits. And he even went to apply for a teaching job down here."

Holly looked surprised. Oh, my God, would that imply he didn't want to repair the marriage? Was Ella giving the wrong version?

"He may be applying to a California school also. You know, he doesn't tell me things like that. He thinks I wouldn't understand." Ella beamed, having arrived in a safety zone.

Holly adjusted the ruffle at the neck of her white blouse. Ella always loved her in white. She looked so soft and virginal and it gave her the aura of a choirgirl. Holly raised an eyebrow.

"Are you sure of this? You know for a *fact* that he made application? He wants to teach?' Holly weighed this information.

"Holly, we talked about it. I know." Ella was firm.

"Look, we've had a difficult time. As the kids get older and less dependent I've become more independent myself, and the only one pulling at my dress has been Donald. He was so indecisive, so dissatisfied with his career, with himself, finally, that I felt he was destroying all the happiness in my life. And in the children's."

"But you love each other," Ella protested.

"Darling, haven't you seen enough movies to know that love is not enough? I'm a joyful person and the girls are very ebullient. Donald is like Mr. Gloom, stamping around the house with a black cloud over his head. It got so I just couldn't stand having him around anymore."

"It breaks my heart." Ella felt the tears flowing.

"Darling, it breaks my heart too." Holly put her arms around Ella. "You believe me when I say I love him. And he does move me. I'm sorry for him. But I can't stand living with him this way. It just won't work. He has to convince me that he's changed before I'll let him come back. And, Mom, I really mean that. No temporary, artificial solutions."

"I did tell you he's earning money from the portraits?"

"Oh, Mom, can you truly believe that painting portraits of your friends is making Donald happy? Fulfilled? Don't you remember the goals he used to have, when he wanted to be a really great painter? Does this sound like the same man?"

"So what happened, Holly, where did it go?"

"Mom, I wish I knew. He did work once, not as much as he should have, maybe, but what he produced was good, so good. You know that. All right, nobody ever recognized it, and a lot of lesser artists who followed the fads became famous. But shouldn't that have simply goaded Donald to work harder, to produce more? Instead he just became quietly embittered, and disgruntled, and finally indifferent, too. But ultimately, Mom, it's just a question of personality. Of simple *bounce*. Except when he's stupidly drunk do you know I haven't even seen Donald *smile* in years?"

What from Ella here but a sigh? So intelligent, her Holly, such a perceptive way of putting. And again breaking her heart.

"So again it's my fault. My failure. The personality."

"Oh, Mom, it's not. What more can you give someone in this world than love? Than support? And who's given Donald more of that than you have?"

How Ella loved this young woman, this *daughter*! Could she make a deal somewhere, maybe, swap Donald for Holly and the girls? Even Ella had to laugh. "Wonderful Holly, I didn't even ask what time you got in. Did you eat? You'd like some cheesecake, maybe? Coffee?"

Holly glanced at her watch. "I have an appointment in

about forty-five minutes. Coffee sounds swell, Mom."

So much pain Ella carried in her breast as they walked. Was there any change in Donald at all, really? Some, yes, she was sure there was some. It would work out, it had to.

So why was Ella suddenly laughing again? Because she hadn't even been aware that Holly was holding her hand, was why. Strolling through the Fontainebleau lobby holding hands with this beautiful young woman, a stranger from out of town. And after a hug at the pool, yet. Carole Cavalcanti should happen by accident to see her, *oy*!

"Oh, Holly, I wish you had more time," Ella said. "So much is going on in my life, so many things to tell. Can you imagine, your old mother-in-law, a dinner I gave? With one homosexual and one lesbian?"

Holly tilted her head, amused and skeptical.

"God's truth," Ella insisted. "Such a world, today. And one thing I promise you. Donald, well, I hope and pray he changes. And he will, he will." Again she laughed. "But will you give him some points, maybe, if his mother changes for him?"

CHAPTER

39

ELLA WAS TRYING TO GET PAMELA AND TOMMY TO COME down to the wedding. Tommy probably wouldn't want to come. He was at the age where he pretended descent from the Hapsburgs and they definitely did not have grandparents in Miami. But her Pammy, she would come. She had called a few days ago and talked to Pam's roommate, Virginia. Told her the whole exciting story about the wedding. Virginia had promised to give Pam the message, but no word from her since. With only two days to go. Disappointing.

Ella walked into the living room. Apple cores, orange skins, cigarette butts, rolled up napkins, stray ashes that hadn't made their target, various coasters which had hosted various glasses of vodka, even yesterday's sox greeted her. She began to distribute the debris to final resting places. There was a knock on the door. Who would want her at this hour?

"Who's there?"

"A wedding present for Ella Sagersdorf," the voice answered. From whom? she thought, unlocking the door.

"Grandma!" The cyclone rushed at her. "Grandma, I'm so happy for you! I can't tell you." So much kissing and hugging that Ella could barely catch her breath. Of course it was Pamela.

"My angel, my darling, come on in." She pulled her granddaughter inside.

"Hey, Grandma, wait, I didn't come alone. This is David. He drove me down here. Can't he come in for such a favor?"

"Of course, David, come right in." She held the door for

this young, blond man with a lot of hair, a mustache, but a nice face, a good, strong Jewish face.

"I was just this minute wondering why you didn't call me back. I spoke to Virginia and then not a word from you. I thought you didn't care."

"Oh, Grandma, how could you think that? I was on a holiday with Sheryl and Jeannette Dennison and we took a ski trip to Stowe. We had a fantastic time. I met David there the very first day. Afraid Jeannette and Sheryl didn't see too much of me. Isn't he divine?"

David blushed. Who wouldn't? This child had all Ella's genes and more. Such energy and such honesty. Maybe, in fact, Pam had more honesty than Ella.

"Grandma, we've come for the wedding and we brought sleeping bags. You won't mind if we crash here? I was sure you wouldn't."

Crash? Bang, you're dead. *Here?* Where? In the kitchen, the bathroom, under the tub? The three of them, these two and Marcia, in the second bedroom? Oh, no, Pamela's boyfriend shouldn't see the mask and the earplugs. You saw the mother, you knew what the daughter would grow up to be. No, that wouldn't work.

"We'll manage, dear." Her joy at seeing Pam washed away all reality. Love, indeed, would find a way. "You kids must be used to dormitory living, right?"

"Oh, we won't go into the room with Mommy, Grandma. David and I can stay in the living room."

"With Donald?"

"Uncle Donnie is here? Did he come for the wedding too? How neat."

"Well, he didn't exactly come for the wedding. He didn't know when he came what was going to happen. See, he and Holly had a little difficulty so he came to . . . well, he came."

"Oh, oh. You've got your hands full, right? The son and the daughter come home to mommy. Grandma, that's a gas, you know that? It isn't real. What do you think, David?"

Should they be airing their dirty linen in front of this stranger? She supposed it would make no difference. Pam the truthful would tell him anything Ella left out. And in the way these young kids had, they would analyze the whole family anyhow.

"It hasn't been too easy for me," Ella confessed. "Your mother and your uncle are not the best of friends. They never got on too well and it's worse than ever. Frankly, they are always fighting. Maybe you can be the peacemaker." Donald would like Pam, who could help it? She exuded good energy, Donald could get his karma back.

"Is Aunt Leah going to take care of the wedding? Tell me where it's going to be and what we can do. Hey, David, why don't you take a shower and I'll go second. You got towels, Grandma?"

Sure she did. Told them to put their bags in her bedroom. They were small enough. It was the sleeping bags, where would she hide those?

David went into the shower and Pam pulled her to the couch. "Let's snuggle and you tell me your troubles, Gran. Let me make it all better. That's why I'm here. Pam Adelson, the Great Fixer."

Well, so she was. Ella was feeling stronger already. Such a bright, electric girl. Such a pleasure. Marcia had done one thing well, that was true. Her kids were marvelous. She told her about Marcia's proposed job in Venezuela.

"Wow, that's far out. I can't imagine my mother in South America. It sounds like a very courageous move."

"It is, it is. But I started blaming myself. Maybe she is just doing this to get out of my hair, Pam. Maybe she really doesn't want to go. . . ."

"Gran, I know my mother. If she doesn't want to go, there's no way to make her go. So please, it isn't your decision. Listen, if it doesn't work out, we'll go pick her up and she can drive back with David. He's pretty good in the sack."

Her granddaughter was saying this to her? They were going

to sit down and discuss the size of penises next, maybe? She'd be damned before she got into that kind of chat with this baby.

"You went to bed with him so fast?"

Pam hooted. "I knew you'd say that, you're so true to form. Actually, yes, it was the first night we met. Why the heck not? It gets rusty if you don't use it."

"Pam!"

"Take it easy. I won't tell your friends. Only Leah, she'd understand."

"Who says she would and I wouldn't? I understand too. What's the big deal, right?"

"Right, but now about you. Did you get a wedding dress? Are you going to be a white bride?"

"Peach."

"What?"

"I'm going to be a peach bride. Or a peach of a bride. We were supposed to go on a honeymoon but it's postponed until April. Passover. In the Holy Land. Won't that be nice?"

"Oh, hey, I might even be there on a dig at that time, Gran. That would be super. But listen, when do I meet what's-his-name?"

"Chip."

"You marrying a young kid? What kind of name is that for an old Jewish man?"

"His real name is Hyman. Hyman Lowe. Hy Lowe." Pammy laughed as she knew Pam would. "So he changed it. Besides, he's from Walla Walla, Washington. No Hymies there, right?"

"What's he like?"

"He's fun. He's kind, intelligent. He reads, he listens, he's interested in the world and in people. He's easy to be with, most of all. He doesn't make a lot of noise. It's peaceful. You don't get so passionate at my age, Pam, but you still have feelings. And I feel strongly, very strongly, about this man.

Whatever years I have left, I'd enjoy spending them with Chip."

"Gran, that's great. But don't leave out the fact that you're also a sexy lady. I understand there are only two eligible males in Miami and you've got one of them. That ain't nothing, ma'am."

"Don't I know that? But it's not my sex appeal, Pam. It's my personality." They both laughed.

"Pam, you think it will work out? He's a total stranger."

"Wasn't Grandpa when you met him?"

"Sure. But I was younger then, more flexible."

"Hey, lady, I've got news for you. You're more flexible now. You changed with the times. I couldn't talk to you this way five years ago. Tell you about my sex life. Sure, you get a little red, it's the years of old-style conditioning. But you listen to me and you don't judge me by your own standards. In fact, little old lady, I get the feeling that you're really proud of me and I like it."

"Sweetheart, you don't know how proud. I'm glad you're mine. And when you do something good and important, I will kvell. And in public, you'd better believe it!"

"David, come on out and let me get in there, I stink!" Pam yelled at the door. It was flung open.

"Okay. I feel great, Mrs. Sagersdorf. Do you have any milk?"

No. She'd have to restock the refrigerator with this new generation in mind. They'd love her health foods, but there were a lot of the newer fads she'd hadn't picked up. Tiger's Milk, Lecithin, what were they all?

"Come in the kitchen, dear. I'll show you where everything is, you'll make yourself at home."

Dinner conversation was somewhat formal. She put a leaf in the table to accommodate everyone. There were six of them, counting Chip. Pam and David chatted away. He was in law school, a bright boy. His father was an art historian and Donald knew of him. Seemed to bring David closer to the family. Marcia was tense.

"I like him, Grandma," Pam said as she closed the door on Chip. "Aren't you getting really excited? The day after tomorrow?"

Excited, maybe. More important, how would she get some of these people out? David and Pam would leave the morning after the ceremony. But she'd heard no further plans from Marcia or Donald. What was doing on the Venezuela thing? Maybe she'd put Pam on the job.

"Dear, have you talked to your mother about Venezuela? Maybe you should bring it up?"

Marcia was across the room on the couch, just staring at the ceiling. Donald and David were now talking football. A player named Orange Juice?

"Hey, Mom, what's this Venezuela gig Grandma mentioned? Is it serious?"

"Yes, it is," Marcia answered. "I should get my tickets on Grandma's wedding day." She turned to Ella.

"I didn't realize it was so definite, Marcia. How soon would you leave? My goodness."

"Did you leave yourself an escape clause?" Pam asked her mother. "You know, in case it's not your cup of tea? You're not stuck down there for a specified time period, are you?"

"I had to agree to three months, with a month's notice. It would be hard to find a replacement any sooner."

"You haven't said how you feel about it, Mommy?"

"Well, I'm exploring my feelings. Grandma knows all about that. I've been in group therapy, sharing my thoughts with these people, and I've had a lot of support. And I'm in a women's group, too." Ella didn't know Marcia had been back to the group. She was glad to hear that.

"They all applaud my independence. I'm just not sure I know what I'm doing, what I'm getting into."

"So you give it a whirl. What's three months, maybe four?

You're back in the States and you've lived in Venezuela. How many people can make that claim?" Pam had a point there. Ella hadn't thought of it. It was an exciting trip however you looked at it, and it wouldn't cost any money. In fact Marcia would get paid. Interesting the way Pam picked up on that. She was something. That kid would go anyplace. Give her a ticket, just a hint of a ticket, and she'd pack her toothbrush and be on her way. Brave. Really brave. Should she bring up Stanley the worm, ask Pam how her father was? She never knew what to do. The answer she hoped for, that he was crushed to death under the wheels of a moving train, she never heard. And she really didn't give a damn how he was. Why he didn't meet his alimony payments, that was another question. Plunge in.

"Pam, dear, forgive me for injecting a sour note, but how is your father?"

"Oh, he's the same as ever, Gran. I've come to terms with him. Just happy to have so much Sagersdorf blood in me. Thanks for that."

"Ma," Marcia cut in, "must you put Pam through this examination?"

"It's okay. I understand Gran. She just wants to know whether he's ever going to pay you alimony again. He probably would, David says, if Mom put a good lawyer on the case. She hasn't done a thing except write letters."

"I may not need his blood money after all," Marcia said. "I'll start a new life without it."

Ella thought the evening should end here. What a tableau. Not a soul fighting. Donald and David chuckling over some football story, Pam and Marcia holding hands on the sofa. Take leave of it now, dear Ella, before reality sets in.

"You going to bed so early, Gran?"

"Sit, sit. I'll see you all in the morning."

Pam ran across for a kiss anyway. "Sexy old thing," she whispered with a twinkle. "Listen, I hope somebody's told you about the birds and the bees?"

"A whack on the tuchas, you deserve," Ella grinned.

So Ella was given one playfully instead, as Pam danced away.

Miracles, she thought in the bathroom. Blessings. Ella Sagersdorf has problems? So when did she count her blessings last?

CHAPTER

40

THE MORNING OF THE WEDDING ELLA AWOKE EARLY. RISE and shine, today's the day. But hark, what sound in yonder bathroom? Pam and David? *Her* bathroom?

Fished for her bathrobe, put it on. Found the scuffs and padded in.

"What's going on?"

They had strung streamers all over the small room. Pink and white, luscious looking paper. Hanging onto the fixture in the middle of the bathroom was a gigantic white wedding bell direct from Woolworth's.

"This is very nice of you."

"There's more, Gran. David is going to be your chauffeur today. He'll take you wherever you have to go. Beauty parlor, the Shiatsu massage. . . ."

She had decided to make an appointment with that little Japanese man. Marcia raved about him so why shouldn't she try it, especially on her wedding day? Instead of a mikvah Ella'd have a Shiatsu. Change with the times. Ritual is as ritual does. She'd pretend it was a deeply religious ceremony. That Mr. Nakamura was the world-renowned Zen Rabbi. Hmm. Ella realized that Hebrew has a lot of "l" sounds. Present a formidable task for Rabbi Nakamura. *Erohaynu merach orum.*

"Hey, Gran, I'm going to prepare the first of the two baths you will have today. According to the ritual of Rabbi Adelson. First, the lemon bath. Tonight, sandalwood."

Everybody is a rabbi. "Why do I need two baths today? I'm not so dirty."

"Wherefore is this night different from all other nights? Just trust me, Gran."

It certainly smelled good. Ella loved scented soaps; lemon and sandalwood were indeed her favorites.

"Did David leave the room?"

"Of course he did. Take off the robe and the nightgown and step right in. I'm going to scrub your back too."

Surely this was paradise. She lay back and allowed the bubbles of lemon to tickle her neck, her nose. Pam handed her a soft washcloth.

"There are some places I can't go, Gran."

Ecstasy. Her wedding night could not be such bliss. Big deal wedding night anyway. So who's a virgin?

"Grandma, you have to wear something old, something new."

"Oh, that's silly, Pam."

"No, it's important. What's old?"

"Me," Ella giggled.

"Come on. For real."

"I have an ecru silk purse from France. It belonged to my mother. Is that old enough?"

"Good. Now the new. I'm going to get you a garter. That will do it. And Mom can lend you a handkerchief, that's borrowed. What's blue?"

"How about the Bible? I have to carry one and mine has a blue leather cover."

"Fine."

"You're going to make me wear a lace garter? Where will you get it? From the sex shop?"

"Don't worry. I'll get you a very dignified one. It will have so much class you'll want to expose yourself to the rabbi."

"Dirty mouth. You've got a dirty mouth and a dirtier mind." Loved this child. Delicious.

"Gran, I want to get Chip something. Just a remembrance.

Think he'd like cuff links? I saw some nice ones with David yesterday."

"Can you pick up something for Miriam too, maybe? I'll pay. That's Chip's daughter. She's staying at the Doral, flew in last night with her husband. I'll leave it to your taste."

Pam was massaging her shoulders. "Now relax and get into yourself. Groove."

"Groove, shmoove. In fact who has time?And it's so quiet out there. Where's Donald?" She walked into the living room, draped in a bath sheet.

"He didn't come home last night. Maybe he's with a woman."

"If he doesn't get back for the ceremony, I swear I'll never talk to him again," Ella muttered. Back into the bedroom, her sanctuary.

"Gran, the doorbell. I'll be right back."

Who now? she thought. Make my day cheerful, please? Today of all days? Serene?

"It was your friend Ida. Just saying not to forget the tea this afternoon with your friends."

Oh, Lord, Ella had. Sylvia, and the canasta crowd. Shirley Mittleman, Bessie Goldstein. The artist's models, the beauties of Bimini Towers. So what else would she forget, maybe?

Move slowly, Ella told herself. Glide today, eh?

David drove her to the beauty parlor. He was a careful driver, Ella took note of that. Thank goodness, something less to worry about. Her granddaughter was not driving with a speed freak.

She left him with a kiss and entered the shop. Mr. Randolph was standing there, arms folded, tapping his foot impatiently. She had never managed to find him busy.

"Hurry, Mrs. S., it's your special day and I'm going to give you the works."

"I'm hurrying," she assured him. He always looked so nervous and so peaked. Never seemed to get a tan.

He put her head on the washing trough. "Well, are you sure you know what you're doing, Mrs. S.?"

"I really think so, Randy. My husband-to-be is a fine man."

"I haven't been married," Randolph continued. She suspected as much but refrained from interrupting. "My parents were, and they were miserable. I can't begin to tell you. If you want to know the truth, the people I know who are happiest are those just living together. Without a marriage ceremony. I thought you were a modern woman, Mrs. S. How come you need a license?"

He had a way of complimenting and taking it away in one stroke. "I am modern. Believe me, Randolph. I pleaded with Mr. Lowe to just live together. But he, you know, he's Pacific Northwest. They don't do things like that out there."

Randolph nodded and wrapped her head in a towel. How come she never had a hairdresser like Warren Beatty in *Shampoo*?

David was waiting in the car, eating a chocolate bar.

"It's not good for your teeth," she told him.

"I know," he said. "But I like it. Do we go to the massage now?"

"That's the next stop," she told him.

She glided out of David's car and into Mr. Nakamura's domain. His voice was soft.

"I turn around, you take off clothes and lie down on mat."

Which she did. Would it have been this easy without her afternoon with Marcia beside Joslyn's pool?

Whereupon instant bliss. Ella lay on her stomach, resting on the rolls of soft flesh which served as a cushion, as his fingers molded her, attacked the backaches, the beginning of arthritis, and made it all better.

"You watch weight, okay?"

"Well, I will if you think I should," she replied.

"Eat plenty wheat germ and fish. Rots of fish. Is good for you. Make you rive rong."

"I *have* lived long, thank you. I'm sixty-five."

She expected him to faint with surprise. "Yes," he responded.

No more words. Little plunks of Japanese music stroked her ears, while Mr. Nakamura pulled toes, fingers, kneaded flesh. Magnificent.

She put fifteen dollars into his outstretched hand when she'd finished dressing. "I'm getting married today," she told him. "I'll be Mrs. Lowe next time I phone you."

"Yes, Mrs. Row, you call me anytime. I make you better."

Angie Locatelli should see Sybil Churchill now.

She settled into her telephone chair and talked with Leah. Was her watch wrong, or could they really have spent forty minutes discussing what Leah would serve at the wedding? When she hung up, she realized she still hadn't seen Donald. She walked back into the living room.

"Pam, did you hear from your uncle? Did he come home and go out again, maybe?"

"No to both questions. But he'll be here, don't worry."

What made Pam so sure? She didn't even know this uncle of hers. If he didn't come, if he didn't show up, Ella would just throw him out, bag and baggage into the street. The nerve. She was getting worked up. How many ceremonies had she asked him to attend in his lifetime? Or, God forbid, had something happened to him?

Ella was biting her lip. Marcia used to warn her about anticipating the worst. She'd had an old friend like that. Minnie Lipschutz. Always looking on the gloomy side. Never slept. If she closed her eyes, heaven help her, a fire could break out and she'd surely smother in her bed. Or a burglar would come in through a window and stab her. She padded through the house all night, would lie down at five A.M. when the sun was coming up, and sleep for about three hours. If you went on a trip, Minnie stayed awake so your car wouldn't crash, or your plane wouldn't distintegrate, or your ship wouldn't hit an iceberg. She spent her days worrying about the traffic flow of friends and relatives. Shopkeepers would rob you blind. Never trust a black person, a Chinaman, a foreigner. Banks were stealing your money, the government was run by an international combine consisting, Minnie was sure, of Peter Lorre, Sidney Greenstreet, and J. Edgar Hoover. Her children finally put her into a nursing home so she'd get some sleep. But Minnie just found more people to worry about. Not only the others in the home, but their families as well. Ella got occasional letters admonishing her to stay away from bombers, buses, and burglars. Poor Minnie. And here was Ella, emulating her. Stop, already.

"Pam, come in and make me feel better," she called into the kitchen.

"Here's a cup of tea, old sweet, and I'll make you feel fine. What's the matter?"

"Aren't you worried about Donald? Maybe something happened to him?"

"Gran, he's a grown person. If something happened, we'd hear from the hospital anyway."

"How would they know he's living here? You think he has a name tag?"

Her point got across. Pam wrinkled her eyes. The movement triggered the lock and the door opened.

"Hi, Mom, sorry I didn't get home last night." Here he was, two arms, both legs, no bandages. And calling her Mom.

"Where were you? I was frantic. I've been ready to call the hospitals and the police stations. . . ."

And what packages was he carrying? "I hope you didn't buy me a wedding present?" So now she was getting angry at him. Mostly for just walking in so casually.

"Ella, I didn't want to let you down tonight. Yes, these are presents for you. And this is a sportjacket for me and a new shirt to wear with it. I bought them with some of the money I made off your friends."

She ran up to him. "Oh, Donnie, that's so nice of you. You cared how I felt. I do want my children to look wonderful. I didn't think of it this morning, but I would have remembered tonight. I'm really proud of you."

Donald was setting aside the packages. Ask where he was last night, should she? Minnie Lipschutz to the bitter end? No, no, he's old enough. Suddenly, in fact, Ella started to grin instead.

"What's so funny?" Pamela asked.

"It never crossed my mind until just this instant. Your uncle Donald is my escort. More, he'll have to give me away, he's the oldest living male in the family. Like the father of the bride. Do you think he realizes the responsibility?"

Even Donald joined in the laughter.

The phone rang. It was the rabbi's wife.

"Ella, listen, I'm sorry to tell you that the rabbi is ill. He has a fever and he can't do the ceremony. Darling, he's so upset, you're so special to him. But don't worry. You won't have to postpone. He made a few calls and we got a wonderful replacement, an old man, a real scholar, from Poland. He'll be terrific. I'm coming to stand in for my husband and to tell him how beautiful you look."

Wonderful. The unknown rabbi presides. From Poland. Right out of the pages of Isaac Singer. What sins, what trials will this Job have suffered? And does he speak English? Maybe Zero Mostel, he'll be like, and we'll all have a good time. I'll worry about it later, Ella thought. Every passing moment made her feel closer and closer to Scarlett O'Hara, a shikseh she'd never before understood.

It was two in the afternoon and she realized that she had not spoken to Chip today. She had an idea. Since his son and daughter were staying at a hotel, why couldn't Donald, Pam, and David stay at Chip's apartment? Then only Marcia would be in the second bedroom. And she wore earplugs.

She dialed his number. No answer. Well, he was probably at the hotel with his daughter. She'd try again, after the tea.

Ida loved parties. She had taken down the china cups which she'd been collecting all these years. Creamer and sugar bowl pre Wedgwood. And on the china plates was every kind of Danish pastry known to man, or woman. Prune, cheese, almond paste, custard, strawberry, raspberry, blueberry, and moon. There were pineapple, apple, peach, pear, and even plain Danish. But most of all there was cinnamon and raisin, the exotica, the pièce de résistance for Jewish women.

The girls were all there. They were happy for her. They would all fantasize the wedding ceremony. Remembrances of things past. Jan Peerce singing. No, Lauritz Melchior. Lohengrin, the Wedding March. Always a band, like Meyer Kantrowitz and the Boro Park Five. Bathed in pink lights, pink tablecloths, pink candles, pink matchbook folders. A pink bandstand with Meyer playing rumbas, pasa dobles, congas, polkas, and finally singing to the sweating dancers, "Ladies and gentlemen, your dinner is served." To sit down at round tables with the cousins and the aunts and the uncles, the men in white satin yarmulkes, the waiters bringing in the first course of fish or a hollowed-out canteloupe groaning with balls of watermelon, honeydew, and other exotic fruits. Then soup with matzoh balls and a greasy chicken or overdone roast beef, depending on the pocketbook of the bride's father. And the Scotch and rye still being poured for the uncles and the male cousins who got drunker and drunker with each course. And the champagne for the aunts and the female cousins who giggled and got up to dance the samba and the rumba with yet younger male cousins while Meyer Kantrowitz crooned "Race Me to the Moon" or "Babalú," then cracked a few jokes when the dancers sat down to steal a piece chicken, a dollop stuffed derma, a roll, another green olive. And it was soon over, the bride and groom changing into traveling clothes and the sober aunts picking up the floral centerpieces to take home so they could wilt after three days on their own kitchen tables.

"Let's drink a toast to our Ella, may God be good to her." Sylvia rose and they all followed suit. Raising their Danish pastry into the air. A toast of cinnamon and raisin. Ella thought it was fitting.

She wished she were a more political person. Her campaign would be to put together a commune of older Jewish women —well, they didn't even have to be Jewish, just older—where they could share a house, each with a separate kitchen. They would have privacy, but they'd be together; always there would be someone around. She'd hire teachers to give courses, driver education, for one. It would be like a sorority house, but better. Ida could keep her china collection, Bessie her copper pots and pans, Shirley her Corning Ware. They'd band together. None of these women were stupid. They read books, they went to movies, they watched TV. Some of them traveled. Some of them had fought to the death in businesses beside their husbands and some had run their own.

Sylvia was standing up. "Ella, we didn't know what to give you and Chip. After all, you have a home and possessions. So we thought and thought and decided to give you this illustrated Bible from Israel. We know it would have special meaning for you."

Ella took the box from Sylvia's hands. Opened it with reverence. Oh, it was so beautiful. Carefully she turned a few pages, awed at the engravings, the fine work and craft that had gone into the production of this book. This book.

"You couldn't have given me a better present. I know Chip will love it as much as I do. And we'll always think of all of you," and her hand swept the room, "whenever we open it."

She was dangerously close to sobbing. Fanny Sussman was the first to sense it, and she sprang to the piano. "Let's get some joy into this afternoon," she called. "We'll sing all the old songs." And, since she had gone to the same public school

as Danny Kaye (One Four Nine is the school for me), she
started with "Minnie the Moocher." And on and on.

By the time Ella left she was drunk with laughter. Shirley
Mittelman had taken over and had been in top form. Singing
like Eddie Cantor and Jolson, doing the Melancholy Baby
joke. Finally one by one they had filed into Ida's bathroom
to pee and thus ended the afternoon.

Nobody was in the apartment. Ella went to the phone again
to call Chip. "Hello?" It was a woman's voice.

"Is this Miriam?" Ella asked.

"No, it's Cathy."

"Cathy?" Not Miriam? "Is Chip there?"

"Oh, you want Chip. Here's the number where he can be
reached." And the woman proceeded to give Ella her own
phone number. Glorious.

"Do you know what hotel his daughter is at?" Ella asked.
She realized in asking that she knew the hotel herself. The
only problem was Miriam's married name.

"Listen, I have to run, the doorbell's ringing. Bye." And
the woman put down the phone.

So who was this? Obviously, there were things about Chip
she didn't know. Ella ran down a mental list of Chip's friends.
And their wives. Not a Cathy in the group.

Could she phone and ask the hotel the name of the couple
who came from Seattle? Could they shoot her for trying? She
dialed.

"May I have the reservations desk, please? Hello, listen, I
know this will sound strange, but my daughter has remarried
and just checked into the hotel with her husband and I can't
remember her new last name." Ella tried a small sob.

"Madam, do you know where they are from or do you have
a hint of the names?"

"Oh, she's Miriam and he's Bob and they're from Seattle
and they arrived this morning."

"Yes, yes. We have a Mr. and Mrs. Robert Gaines from Seattle."

"That must be them. Do you have a room number?" Gaines. Probably used to be Goldberg. A cousin of Sidney George Cohen.

Ella thanked the clerk and herself for the quality of their mutual ingenuity and got the room. Nobody there. Maybe they were taking a swim. She left a message and went inside to lie down.

She must have slept soundly for she was being pummeled by a persistent Pam who kept saying, "Gran, hurry."

She looked at the clock. Five. How did it get to be so late? She jumped out of bed.

"I've got the sandalwood bath waiting. Let me put this net over your hair."

Ella felt like a toy doll and let herself be arranged and assembled by Pamela.

"Mom is ready, and Donald is dressing now. Come on, let's get it moving."

She was baptized in sandalwood, sprinkled with bath oil, dried with a huge towel, and led back into the bedroom.

"Gran, I've laid out the clothes on the bed. I'll be your dresser. Like in the theater."

Everything was okay to Ella. She shifted, was tugged at, and found herself standing in front of the long mirror in her peach wedding outfit. It was then she remembered she had still not talked to Chip all day.

"Chip?"

"Oh, he called while you were sleeping. Said nothing important, he'd see you at Leah's. And to remember that he loved you."

"Thank you."

And meanwhile, all the unfinished problems? Oh, well, Marcia would probably leave for Venezuela in a day or so, and Donald could start looking for a place the moment he confirmed the teaching job. She would talk to Chip after the ceremony, at least they'd be sending three of the brood to his apartment for tonight.

The five of them bundled into the car. Ella in the front seat with David, and Donald, Marcia, and Pam in the back.

"Ella," Donald asked, "who's the stand-in rabbi?"

"What's the difference?" Marcia snapped. "The ceremony is legal whoever the rabbi."

"I'm just asking, for Chrissakes," Donald replied.

Silence seemed best for Ella. Close the ears, just keep the eyes open to find Leah's apartment building and say here it is to David. Riding that way, the trip seemed very brief.

Chip, Miriam, and Bob were already there. How handsome Chip looked. He was wearing a new seersucker jacket and gray trousers. His tie was gray, his eyes were gray-blue. They were smiling at her.

"Ella darling, this is my daughter, Miriam, and her husband, Bob."

"Welcome to the family," Miriam said. Bob nodded. They were equal in stature and in looks. Both redheads, both brown-eyed, pale skin, square frames. They look like twins, Ella thought.

"These are mine," and she gestured, "my son, Donald, and my daughter, Marcia. My granddaughter Pamela and her friend David."

"You look gorgeous!" That was Leah's voice and Ella turned. Leah herself was luscious in lemon. Now they were two little fruits, the friends, juicy and color-coordinated.

"Where's the rabbi?" Donald asked. So much concern for the rabbi. Maybe Donald was becoming a religious fanatic. Could he make a living at that, maybe?

"Five, ten minutes at the most he'll be here," Irving said.

"Chip, can we talk a minute?"

Ella tugged at him and they slipped into Leah's bedroom.

"Listen, I haven't been completely successful with the *kinder.* Another few days, maybe, maybe a week. So it occurred to me, we can send Donald and my granddaughter and David to your place to sleep for tonight, say, and . . ."

"*Oy.*" Chip looked pained. Truly pained.

"What *oy?*" Ella asked him.

"Ella, a commitment should be strong, right?" he asked.

"Of course it should. What does that mean?"

"Well, I didn't want to leave a maybe. I didn't want to have a place to go back to, if necessary. Ella, I put the furniture into storage and I sublet the apartment to Murray Baron's daughter Cathy. She moved in today. There *is* no apartment for Donald and Pamela and David tonight. Do you understand?"

Did she understand? Ella wasn't even sure whether she was laughing or weeping. Chip's kids were considerate enough to stay at a hotel, hers would be with them on their wedding night.

"Ella, are you all right? Is that a problem?"

"Problem, shmoblem. So we'll have a party, we'll worry about it tomorrow. Is that the doorbell? Is it the rabbi?"

Evidently it was. Ella started out, Chip following. The rabbi from Poland, a refugee. Maybe they'd invite him, too.

Rabbi Waldman's wife was just entering, leading the smallest man Ella had ever seen. Rabbi Tom Thumb also had a beard which seemed to reach to his knees. The beard was as pointed as his little black shoes which peeked out from beneath his baggy, and shiny, blue pants.

"Rabbi Moshe Lieberman." Mrs. Waldman intoned the name. The entrance was not complete, Ella noticed. Behind them, equally small in stature but rounder in form was, she supposed, the rabbi's assistant. He was carrying a beach umbrella. A beach umbrella?

"I'm Shloime Katz," he announced gaily, extending his hand to the gathering. At least he spoke English. Well, a kind of English. He looks like the Reverend Moon. A Jewish Moon. Tweedledee Moon, round rabbi's helper.

"All set, ready to go?" the rabbi questioned. The congregation strained to hear. He had a thin voice, like a defective flute. "Shloime will put up the chupah."

Of course, we need a canopy. Ella was not prepared for the umbrella opening, however. She groaned. There it was, her wedding canopy unfurled. Announcing *Schwartz Kosher Motel/Apartments. Swimming Pool.*

What could Miriam be thinking? Her father, fresh from the West Coast, lost in this ghetto. Couldn't Shloime have at least found one from the Doral or the Fontainebleau?

"You got the ring, the wineglass to break?" Shloime was obviously the stage manager. Tom Thumb was saving himself for the ceremony. Leah ran into the kitchen for a wineglass. Maybe she could find an old Snow White and the Seven Dwarfs cottage cheese glass. Perfect, under the circumstances.

Everyone clustered around the umbrella as if to get in out of the rain. Tom Thumb took off his yarmulke and produced a little top hat. Class at that, Polish magic. Yet nice, Ella had to admit.

"Hyman?" Of course, he couldn't call him Chip. "Ella?" He pointed again. Arrange the players. Shloime got into position behind the rabbi. Leah and Irving were the attendants. She supposed Irving had the ring. Leah pulled the veil down over Ella's face. Was all this going well or badly? Ella wasn't sure.

The rabbi began his litany. A flute solo on a broken flute. Up and down he trilled, who knew what wondrous words were being voiced? He was fascinating to watch. That diminutive person with his tiny voice, rocking back and forth, head bobbing, blessing everybody. She recognized some of it, knew he had not yet taken up the question of marriage. Probably get to it after the seven deadly sins. Then Shloime began a chant. The marriage banns. Rabbi Lieberman poked and pulled at Chip and at her. He yipped at Irving, who produced the ring after all. Ella and Chip kissed and walked out from under *Schwartz Kosher Motel/Apartments. Swimming Pool.* To find themselves united as man and wife.

This was not like the Jewish weddings of the past. This was different. Miriam, Bob, Donald, Marcia, Pam, David, even Mrs. Waldman, were proper, almost Waspish. Thank goodness for Tom Thumb and the Reverend Moon, who made the ceremony seem at least remotely authentic. Ella and Leah hit the champagne bottle immediately, tipping it into their glasses several times in a minute. Giggling. The rabbi had eaten his chopped liver on cracker (Saltine), packed up his belongings, and fled back to wherever. The rest of them were going to sit down at Leah's big table and eat filet mignon. Ella was married? This was it?

Still, the table looked gorgeous. Leah was in top form as well. On one side of Ella sat Miriam, the new daughter. She'd better plunge right in and try to cement this relationship.

"Dear, you have such good taste. I love the way you decorated your father's apartment." Uh-oh, or shouldn't a single woman be visiting a man's apartment? "He had some people over and I was so impressed," Ella improvised.

"I love to do that, Ella. During tax season, Robert gets so busy, and several years back I decided to try my hand at professional decorating. Lo and behold, if it wasn't a fabulous success. My reputation spread and I can't seem to get a minute off."

How come other people's children seem to find work, seem to make money? And Miriam didn't even need the money. From what Chip told her, Bob was a very successful accountant.

"For myself, I'm retired totally," Ella laughed. "It will just be fun to spend time together with your father."

"He does adore you, Ella. And I want you to know that I'm very pleased that he's found this companionship. Robert and I feel relieved, yes, quite so, having met you."

Who did she think her father was going to marry, a seventeen-year-old cheerleader? Can't she give him a little credit? Miriam was nice, Ella felt, but just a little too smug.

"Your father is a remarkable man, Miriam. We have a tremendous lot that we share together."

"I wish we could have brought the children for you to meet. I know they'd like you. But Dad said he will be bringing you to Seattle in a few months. And you must get to know Walla Walla."

And all the memories of your mother. "I'm looking forward to that."

"Ella, I was very close to both my parents. We had a very affectionate relationship. It may sound crazy to you, but I know my mother would have liked you."

Ella fought back the tears. "Miriam, that is a lovely thing to say. I choose to believe I would have liked her, too. I can't take the place of your mother for you, I know, but I can promise to love and cherish your father as you'd like me to."

Ella looked around the table. Bob was talking to Donald. They seemed to be getting on well. Marcia interrupted and Donald didn't snap at her. They must have agreed on a truce. Panmunjom. Pam was beaming from across the way, and Chip squeezed Ella's hand from the side opposite Miriam. He'd be squeezing more than her hand tonight. Ella Nathanson Sagersdorf Lowe.

Ella who?

Gevalt. Now *gevalt.* It had happened, after all!

Two cars were needed to carry them back to what, absurdly, Ella thought of as the honeymoon suite. It was only when she found a minute alone in her bathroom that it occurred to her, why hadn't she and Chip taken a hotel room for the night? Except how could you find one without reservations at this time of year?

"How does everybody feel about one last brandy before we turn in?" Chip was asking. Or was he pleading? Pam and David looked wide awake, Donald was clutching a freshly poured three or four ounces of vodka, and Marcia, oh, well, who could read Marcia when she was just looking sour?

"Great idea!" Ella was the only one to second the motion. Chip handed her a rather large brandy. Obviously expressing his mood. She prayed for the Red Sea to open and swallow up these interlopers. Instead, wide awake or not, Pam was suddenly unrolling two sleeping bags near her bedroom door. *Oy*, and Marcia yawning now over there also.

So what's this, on top of everything the doorbell blasting like the building is on fire? Who, when we're all here? Ella couldn't move.

Donald went to the door. Nu, so why not, so didn't he live here now too? Didn't everybody?

In he bounded, screaming. "Grandma!"

Tommy? And so big? Ella forgot everything, dashing across. Again the hugging, the kissing, her heart could burst.

"I tried to make the ceremony, but we got hung up. In stupid Georgia yesterday, of all places!"

We? Oh, yes, indeed, shyly, right behind him. Tall, lanky, red-haired, a beauty. "Grandma, Ma, this is Susan. Listen, I had to lay out practically my last dime to fix that stupid car. In fact we're starved. Can I assume you're still celebrating? Can I assume we can stay here with you for tonight?"

It took an hour. For the backs to be slapped, the cheeks kissed, the hands wrung. And of course the new eating. So, another two, Ella decided, who would notice? Let them "crash" too. Bang, boom.

Somewhere along the line she lost Chip, however. Where? In her bedroom. Just hanging up the phone as she entered.

"Ella, pack a bag."

"What pack? And for where?"

"Ella, don't argue with Hyman Lowe on your wedding night!" He meant this? No, delightfully the stern look turned into a grin. "Would you believe the finest suite in the hotel? Two rooms, overlooking the ocean? Unfortunately, it's only available for one night."

Ella hugged him. And hugged him. "One is wonderful. Tomorrow we'll worry. And if tomorrow was good enough for Scarlett O'Hara, why not for us?" She turned to start packing, glanced back. "But you didn't even say. Where is this miracle, by the way?"

Chip was laughing and laughing. "Where else? The Schwartz Kosher Motel and Apartments. With swimming pool."